"I don't take rejection well, Elena. I'm going to take you on a slow journey, no detours or shortcuts."

They were engulfed in symphonic ecstasy, pressing skin to skin, wrapping themselves in the moist heat from their bodies. Dave's hands began a thorough exploration of the secret depths of her body, causing Elena to gasp with turbulent desire.

"You, David Atwell, are not going to make me think that we are meant as a duet. I am a soloist and have been since we said good-bye twelve years ago. I will continue to be a soloist after you abandon your attempts to woo me with your sensuous night music."

"Wrong, Elena," he breathed huskily. "We are a duet . . . I will be your piano. You can practice your finger exercises on me as long as you like!"

Dear Reader,

It is our pleasure to bring you a new experience in reading that goes beyond category writing. The settings of **Harlequin American Romance** give a sense of place and culture that is uniquely American, and the characters are warm and believable. The stories are of "today" and have been chosen to give variety within the vast scope of romance fiction.

It is commonly known that men are more romantic than women. This fact is proven in the charming and poignant story of David Atwell and Elena Shubert. Elena, a concert pianist, has been cloistered from the outside world. David, in his overpowering love for her, cracks her veneer and gently leads her into the world of love, romance, and passion. Andrea Davidson has truly spun a tale that we will long remember.

From the early days of Harlequin, our primary concern has been to bring you novels of the highest quality. **Harlequin American Romance** is no exception. Enjoy!

Vivian Stephens

Vivian Stephens
Editorial Director
Harlequin American Romance
919 Third Avenue,
New York, N.Y. 10022

Music in the Night

ANDREA DAVIDSON

Harlequin Books

TORONTO • NEW YORK • LONDON
AMSTERDAM • PARIS • SYDNEY • HAMBURG
STOCKHOLM • ATHENS • TOKYO • MILAN

"Harmonies are like enlacing arms;
the melodies are the necks we kiss,"
Claude Debussy

Published July 1983

First printing May 1983

ISBN 0-373-16016-X

Printed in Canada

Chapter One

Dave tugged with an index finger at the stiff collar of his white dress shirt in an attempt to loosen the starched stranglehold on his neck. Trying to lift the expression of misery from his face, he only succeeded in raising it to the level of discomfort.

He felt like a misplaced lumberjack, since he stood at least a head, and was twice the breadth in shoulder, above everyone else waiting to enter the concert hall. And too he was afraid he was sweating as much in his formal attire as he ever had in his jersey during the most rigorous game. Beyond that, he was bored.

He looked at his date and yawned. Oh, she was gorgeous, all right. A cool blonde, slim and leggy—and vacuous.

"So how long have you been modeling?" he asked in an indifferent monotone.

"Since I was seventeen," she cheerfully effused, oblivious of Dave's eyes rolling back in his head.

The crowd finally began to surge forward into the auditorium, relieving the tiresome ache in his left leg from maintaining one position for so long. He had been flanked by his luscious blond model and the date of his friend Jerry Monroe for at least half an hour while they waited for the throng of symphony lovers to enter the hall. The conversation had been primarily one-sided as Jerry regaled them all with his rather unorthodox investment philosophy.

But as the usher helped him find his seat, Dave realized he was no better off than he had been in the lobby. The seat was much too small for his large frame and too close to the one in front of it for his long legs. If only he could drape his calves over the back of the seat in front of him. He glanced wryly at his date. Well, no. Undoubtedly she would find that blatantly uncouth.

To relieve his mind of the discomfort he was feeling, he focused his attention on the grandeur of the hall and the rather ostentatious wherewithal of the patrons surrounding him. Most of the women in the audience refused to shed their furs for fear someone might overlook their nouveau-riche status. Gentlemen sat stiffly next to their wives and looked miserable, as if they would much rather be home watching Monday night football.

The interior design of the building was a synthesis of true beauty and glittering display. The walls of the auditorium were pale blue brocade, divided into redundant rectangles by statues of Apollo, Orpheus, Linus, Ligeia, the nine Muses, and other lesser-known dieties who had found delight or sustenance through music.

Flames of light flared from the crystal prisms of immense chandeliers and danced capriciously across the walls and floor.

The warmth and unreality of the room hovered around Dave, providing a sense of shelter that insulated him against the winter world outside where big, wet flakes of snow were falling, and immediately melting, against the building.

The music hall was one of the few old buildings in

the downtown area that had been unscathed by the path of progress. Some purification-minded reformists labeled it a white elephant, a symbol of the decadence and excessiveness of pre-Depression days.

But to David Atwell it was a monument to days gone by, days that were perhaps softer and more manageable, to times when a man had fewer difficult decisions to make. When the world was like a wheel that kept constantly and evenly turning. Perhaps then all a man had to do was take his place on the wheel and ride out his days in a consistent pattern without worry of what tomorrow might bring.

And too the concert hall was a reminder of his adolescence, when his parents would force him to sit through countless symphonies, hoping to instill in him a modicum of sophistication and culture.

They would glance down at their young son, an expression of omnivorous absorption on his face, and they would never know that his thoughts were a lightyear away from the symphonic composition being performed.

Instead, his mind would be wandering through the applicability of lateral passes, off-tackle maneuvers against a split defense, touchdowns, and extra points.

Now, after all these years in the National Football League, he had come home. Home. What a strange connotation that word had for him. He had been on the move for so long, traded from one team to another, one city to another, making his home wherever he happened to be.

This city was as unfamiliar now as any other had been. His parents had moved to Florida after his father retired. His brother and sister had both married their college sweethearts and were living at opposite ends of the country. And yet, this city, only an hour from New York, was different from all the others. It was where he had first learned to catch a football from his father. It was where he had learned the fundamentals of survival, of sportsmanship, of the competitive edge. It was where he had grown to be a man.

Home. Yes, he decided, it had a nice ring to it.

His blond date realigned her willowy body in her seat, seductively sliding a red spiked fingernail down the sleeve of Dave's coat. He returned an indulgent smile, then berated himself for his cool response. *Look at her, man. She's gorgeous! And here you are all alone in a new town. Don't be an ass.*

He covered her hand with his own, trying to generate genuine desire in his response.

The agglomeration of incongruous sounds emitting from the orchestra, as the individual members tuned their instruments to perfection, was beginning to taper off. Finally each musician assumed his place and adjusted his sheet music, and the lights of the magnificent music hall dramatically dimmed.

The silver-haired conductor, dressed elegantly in black tails, walked out onto the stage and bowed once before the audience, then turned and nodded to his orchestra.

As soon as he was standing before his musicians, the piano soloist glided across the stage in her unadorned long black dress, the heels of her dark pumps tapping rhythmically against the glazed wooden floor. She seated herself gracefully on the hard piano bench and immediately turned her face toward the conductor for her cue.

The minute she walked on stage, David's breath lodged tortuously in his throat. Without realizing what he was doing, his fingers closed tightly over those of the woman beside him, causing her to gasp with pain and withdraw her hand.

Dave grimaced apologetically as he looked at his date. "I'm sorry, Georgia. I didn't mean to. . ."

He lifted his gaze back to the stage and stared. His eyes were trained intensely on the woman at the piano. Twelve years. Could it really be her?

He held the program up close to his eyes and, despite the darkness, quickly scanned it for her first piece.

Rachmaninoff's Concerto No. 2 in C Minor. Soloist—Elena Shubert. It really was her. He smiled, expelling a long, tremulous breath.

His thumb began absently stroking the printed letters that spelled out her name on the program while his thoughts tumbled back across the years, gathering the bits and pieces of memories that had, after so many years, lingered with such crystal clarity.

Elena's long, tapered fingers lifted from her lap and hovered in anticipation over the ivory keys of the glossy black concert grand.

A hush fell over the dimly lit room. Not only could one hear the proverbial pin drop, but the silent void was so profound that it emptied each soul and left it breathlessly waiting to be filled with the ethereal music of heaven. In that brief, still moment Dave heard soft patters against the windows where flecks of whirling snow pelted the transparent glass.

As the first chord of the Rachmaninoff concerto was struck, the walls of the auditorium began to reverberate and swell with the deep pathos and dark struggle of the composer's native Russia.

Dave's chest felt as if it would explode, not so much from the sweeping intensity of the music and the skillful playing, as from Elena's presence. His memory had not failed him. She was as captivating as he had remembered. If only he had known she was with this symphony, he would have made sure his seat was closer to the stage where he could see her better. Yet, even from here, her piquant features, her translucent, alabaster skin, and her thick chestnut hair, now coiled at the back of her head, were just as he had remembered them.

Elena's eyes closed briefly as her fingers glided across the keyboard in a moving sostenuto passage, and Dave's thoughts flitted back to that night so long ago when she had closed her eyes with him. To the memory of her body so trustingly his. The remembrance of her hands touching his skin. On that cold winter night the innocent scent of honeysuckle that always seemed to linger around her had filled his youthful head with a feeling of omnipotent power and virility he had never known since. Her soft face had been provocatively framed by the moonlight and that rippling mass of hair had disturbed his senses in a way he could hardly contain.

Dave's mind listened with rapt wonder to the whispers of the past while the sometimes heroic, sometimes nostalgic melody of the concerto floated through its three movements.

Elena's playing was effortless and sensitive. He had to admit, she was where she had wanted to be. This had been her dream. They had both had their dreams,

Dave remembered all too well. Their first loves. And they had both followed paths that were not destined to cross.

The concerto came to a close, and Dave's fragile reflections were broken into shards by the thunderous applause. Elena stood and gracefully bowed at her thin waist to the approving audience. Without a second glance at that instrument that had responded so eloquently to the tips of her fingers, she exited the stage.

Dave tensed. Maybe he should go backstage and try to see her. Just to say hello. Yet, could he wait for intermission? *No!* an inner voice shouted. *Go see her now!*

He unwound his good leg, the one that had not been permanently twisted inside from numerous injuries on the playing field, and leaned sideways to tell his date and his friend Jerry Monroe that he would return in a few minutes. Before he could verbalize his explanation, the orchestra swept into its next piece.

Shifting to a lighter tone, the musicians were now playing Bizet's "March of the Toreadors" from the *Carmen Suite*. Half untangled from his position, Dave realized with annoyance that he was stuck. Rather than leave during the middle of a piece, he would simply have to wait until intermission.

The orchestra played two more short pieces, a pleasant Mendelssohn air and a lighthearted Strauss waltz, before the lights flooded the auditorium for intermission. By that time Dave's body was so cramped in the small confines of the chair that he wondered if he would be able to stand at all.

"Where are you going, Atwell?" Jerry asked as he watched Dave unwind his long legs.

"The piano soloist. I know her." His voice was shaking with an excitement that was curiously enough like that of an adolescent. "I thought I'd go back and say hello. I'll be back in just a—"

"Great!" Jerry boomed. "We'll go with you." He was already standing and pulling his date up with him, unaware of Dave's mild irritation over the intrusion. Knowing he couldn't very well tell them to stay here, he reluctantly took his own date's hand and helped her into the aisle. The four of them began making their way down the aisle against the flow of traffic. They opened the side door below and to the left of the stage and climbed the winding stairway to the wings.

The scene before them was a state of controlled chaos. Members of the orchestra, dressed uniformly in black, stretched their limbs and sipped at steaming mugs of coffee. Nervous stagehands hovered anxiously around sound equipment, adjusting speaker balance or tonal ranges and fitfully wringing their hands over a malfunctioning tweeter.

Dave and his friends moved purposefully through the crowd, then stopped on the fringe of a small group clustered around the conductor and several of the musicians. Dave pulled in a quick chain of breaths and drank in the sight of Elena Shubert, who shined like a singular entity of light among that globular cluster.

He stared at her for a long moment, capturing the essence of her beguiling charm and comparing it with that of the eighteen-year-old girl he had known so long ago.

She had a more mature look about her, her eyes lacking that brilliance of innocence. And yet, she was still as fascinating as ever.

Her lips were drawn together tightly, turning downward slightly in a melancholy crescent, and Dave smiled within himself, as if by doing so he could psychically induce a similar response in her.

Elena glanced up, registering the presence of this large man who was staring at her. People were always coming backstage to meet the musicians and procure autographs. And normally she was more than happy to sign their programs or encourage a young aspiring music student. After all, she too had been in the same position at one time, on the outer fringe of the music world, hoping and striving for a chance to join the elite ranks of the professional musician.

But tonight she had no time for anyone. Her nervous system was strung as tightly as piano wire, and she continually wiped her damp palms on her handkerchief, trying to remove at least the more obvious signs of nervous tension.

Since her manager had warned her of the competition she now faced, her self-confidence had been slowly eroding, and she knew that the next few performances could be crucial to her future.

She tried to follow the conversation going on around her, but too many concerns of her own were interfering with her concentration. She kept hearing the warning of her agent over and over. She kept thinking about how important these next few performances were going to be. Would all of her years of knocking at the same door come to naught?

She felt the heat from someone's unwavering gaze and she glanced again at the man and his friends standing at the edge of the circle of people. Embarrassed by such an intense stare, she tried to focus her attention on the conductor, who was now discussing a minor change in the second half of the performance.

Something pricked at a spot in the back of her mind. An electrical impulse darted through the circuitry of memory, and she looked up in amazement at the man who had been staring at her. She stared back. It had to be a mirage, a trick of her mind. Surely fate did not work in such twisted ways.

Two of the palest green eyes she had ever known were searching her face for recognition. His brown hair was impeccably styled, a fact she couldn't help but notice because it was so out of character for the boy she had once known. Back then his hair had seemed to have a life of its own and he had never been able to control its wild abandon.

It was like him in a way. She had never been able to control him, nor would she have wanted to. David Atwell had had his own life to live, his own path to walk, and no one, including herself, would ever be able to tame him.

Dave smiled at Elena, fully aware that she now recognized him and was remembering those innocently passionate nights so long ago. Though it was a boyish smile, full of adolescent familiarity and youthful memories, it also carried with it a touch of intimacy that both bewildered Elena and, at the same time, electrified her.

"Yes?" She tore her eyes away from the man and the memory when she realized that Alexi had been speaking to her. "I'm sorry, what did you say?"

The maestro glared down at her disdainfully. "I was saying that you must remember to pick up the tempo slightly in the Prokofiev, the way we discussed this afternoon."

Elena was nodding her head slowly, but her response was obviously not adequate enough for Alexi. "Do you think you can manage that?" he asked condescendingly.

Elena bristled at the supercilious tone he was using with her in front of the other musicians. "I understand perfectly, Mr. Zsarkof," she ground through clenched teeth, then stood and bowed perfunctorily to him. "Now, if class is over, I would like some fresh air." The emphasis on the word *fresh* left no doubt in anyone's mind that she found Alexi Zsarkof's air to be on the unpleasantly stale side.

She walked out of the circle of people on the opposite side from where Dave and his friends were standing.

"Hey, I thought you said you knew her," Jerry called out to Dave's back as it politely shoved its way through the standing-room-only crowd and moved toward Elena's rapidly retreating figure.

"Elena!" Dave called from behind her. Catching up with her, he grasped her elbow and spun her around to face him. "Elena? Don't you recognize me? Dave Atwell," he prompted, trying to elicit some familiar response from her. He had seen that look of recognition in her eyes a moment ago. He had seen that and more. And yet, now she was acting as if she didn't know him.

"Hello, David. Of course I remember you." She smiled politely, if coolly, and the large hand that had grasped her arm was dropped to his side. He stepped back, more than a little bewildered by her lack of enthusiasm at seeing him.

Schooling her expression into one of refined politeness, she gazed up at the arresting, self-assured face with its tan, implacable features. It was an older face, more time-etched and leathery, but it still held the same immovable granite strength that it had when he was twenty.

His was an athletic face, one whose features had borne the brunt of harsh physical contact. Yet, she still remembered how surprised she was by the way that same countenance could soften in moments of tenderness, his gentle green eyes lit with affection and his tantalizing smile tugging at some restless longing within her.

As she had done twelve years ago, Elena quickly forced a shutter down over those unbidden memories. She had been only eighteen when she met him, yet she had known instinctively that she had to stay away from David Atwell. To accomplish what she wanted in life Elena learned early the price she would have to pay. She had known, at eighteen, that there would never be room in her life for a boy like David.

And now, with career uncertainty looming menacingly before her, she certainly didn't have room in her thoughts for physical longings from the past. She was a disciplined person and she had learned long ago what that meant in terms of personal relationships. She definitely knew better today than to toy with the possibilities David could offer as a man.

"I hope you'll excuse me, David. I was going outside for some fresh air. It was really nice seeing you again," she added on a final note. She took two steps to the exit, then opened the door and started to walk down the stairs into the alley. But she immediately halted as the wet snow lashed at her face, and quickly closing the door, she sighed a slow breath of fatigue.

Accepting the fact that she would have to endure the stuffy heat of backstage, Elena turned back around and was immediately charged with a blistering indictment from David's eyes.

"Is that all you have to say to me?" he challenged. " 'It was nice seeing you'?"

"I beg your pardon?" Elena replied, mystified by his anger.

"Elena!" He frowned. "Dave Atwell, University of Missouri, twelve years ago, you were a freshman, I was a junior, we were—"

"What do you want, David?" she interrupted quickly before he could remind her of what they had once been to one another.

"Well, a little polite conversation would be nice."

Elena's gaze lifted over David's shoulder. The other musicians were filing back onto the stage and Alexi was signaling to her with impatience.

"I'm sorry, David. I have to go on now. I—"

"What about after the concert?" he asked eagerly. Her mind now trained on the second half of the evening performance, Elena looked at him blankly, not comprehending his request.

"My friends and I are going to a resturant," he explained, "and we'd like for you to come along."

Elena glanced at David's slinky lady friend and noticed anything but welcome in her glare. She certainly didn't appear as if she wanted Elena to go anywhere with them.

"I've had dinner," Elena answered.

"We're also going to a bar for drinks. We could talk about old times, reminisce a little." He touched her upper arm deliberately, and his fingers, like huge steel tines, left a marked sensory imprint through the fabric of her dress.

"I don't drink, David. But thank you for the invitation," she lied with a smile. "Excuse me, but I have to go on now."

Dave loosened his hold on her arm and, in a bewildered daze, stepped aside to let her pass. As she walked past him the hem of her black dress brushed lightly across the toe of his shoe, and the sweet scent of honeysuckle wafted upward, touching his nose.

"I thought you said you knew her," Jerry complained again. "Real nice friends you have, Atwell."

A spasm of loneliness swept through Elena's bones as she walked toward Alexi, and with it came an annoying physical hunger for this man she had not seen for twelve years nor ever thought she would see again. And yet, it was more than the memory of them together that tugged at her now. It was the living presence of him in the here and now.

Raising herself up to her full five feet four inches, she sharply reprimanded herself. *It's an itch, Elena. Nothing more than a physical yen that will go away.*

Stiffening her perfectly straight spine, she walked through a chorus of applause onto the stage behind the conductor, entering the arena that was her life.

"I had forgotten how cold this city could get in the winter." Dave huddled inside his coat, the collar turned up against the wind, his hands thrust deeply into the pockets.

"What are you doing here, David?" Elena asked in a tone of exasperation. She was bundled tightly in a red fox coat, the color blending perfectly with the russet highlights of her hair. They were both standing on the wide marble stairway that led down from the concert hall to the sidewalk, she two steps higher than he.

"Waiting for you."

"I thought I said I would not be joining you and your friends," she answered tightly, her mouth compressed into a solid line against the chill. Several strands of hair had fallen loose from beneath her hat and were swirling in wild animation around her face.

"My friends have gone."

"Your girl?"

"My girl—" Dave smiled at her quaint use of the word "—has gone too. My friend Jerry took her home."

"Oh." The cold air had brought a flush to her cheeks and Dave had a difficult time restraining his hand from reaching up to touch her rose-tinged skin.

"You know, my friends were convinced that I lied about knowing you." He frowned at her critically. "I think you could possibly use a lesson in manners."

"I was in the middle of a performance," she answered sharply, then began walking down the stairs at a right angle to this infuriating and persistent man. She had no room for his presence in her life. He was a memory from the past—nothing more.

"Oh, that explains it," he retorted sarcastically. "Where are you going?" He caught up with her in one stride and grasped the thick fur warming her upper arm.

"I'm going home, David." She looked at his face, then quickly averted her gaze, afraid to stare too long into those pale olive-green eyes.

"Can you spare the time for a cup of coffee? Or don't you drink that either?"

Her eyes flicked to his mouth and eyes, trying to determine if he was being facetious. He was smiling.

She sighed philosophically. "There is an all-night café not far from here." Not giving her the chance to change her mind, Dave immediately clasped her gloved hand in his and began leading her down the street.

The wind was swirling the wet flakes of snow around them, striking their faces with sharp stings. And in the cold dark night Elena couldn't be sure but she thought she detected a slight limp in his stride.

"Where do you live?" The chill politeness of Elena's voice crackled in the below-freezing air, arcing upward in a short cloud of night vapor.

"I've been living in Texas for the past few years, but I've made a career change and I've decided to move home. I'll be taking the train to New York City once or twice a week. However—" he shivered "—I think I've become soft in my old age. This weather is going to take some getting used to."

"You'll be living here?" Elena asked, her breath now sending out agitated clouds of fog.

"Well, I certainly don't intend to fly all the way to New York from Dallas every week. Is there something wrong with my living here?"

"No." She felt an apprehensive tremor in the pit of her stomach. "I just wondered. What kind of work are you going to be doing?" she asked, forcing her voice to remain casual.

"I'll be working in television," he answered, listening to the words as they rolled across his tongue. It was still so new and different from the life he had known for so many years. "God, I sound like a pompous ass!" He laughed. "I'll be working in television," he repeated with an exaggerated British accent. "Actually, I'm going to be a sports announcer."

"Oh. How nice," Elena replied falsely. "I don't have time to watch much television, other than some of the concerts on the public station. I'm sure that will be lots of fun for you." Her hand was freed from his grasp and she shoved it into her pocket and lowered her chin against a sudden gust of cold air.

She stopped, realizing that David was no longer beside her. Turning around, she saw him about ten feet behind her, staring at her as if she were something that had escaped from the zoo.

"I was wrong," he said. "You are the pompous ass."

"I beg your pardon!" she huffed.

"Don't beg my pardon, Elena Shubert." Dave stalked up to her, towering over her much shorter and slighter frame. He lowered his face so close to hers that their breaths were intermingling and, in exaggerated ritardando tones, repeated, "You are a pompous ass."

Elena's chin jutted forward and her eyes crinkled arrogantly. But Dave stood his ground, the set of his eyes and mouth daring her to argue, and she finally lowered her chin, her gaze dropping down to his wet black dress shoes.

"I'm sorry, David." She cleared her throat to fill the void of not knowing what to say next. She really hadn't meant to sound so high and mighty. Something about his presence here tonight brought out this defensive, isolationist attitude in her. But she would have to watch her tone of voice. After all, David was an old . . . friend.

Dave could tell that the apology had been a difficult gesture for her, so he didn't press for more. He draped his arm across her shoulder casually and resumed walking down the sidewalk. "You said you knew of a place close by to get a cup of coffee," he reminded her. "My only conclusion is that you are sadistic to the core or your sense of distance is lots different from mine."

"Are you that cold?" Elena laughed lightly, relieved that the tension of a moment earlier had dissolved. "You really have gotten soft in your old age. There is where we're going." She pointed to a warmly lit café across the street. "Do you think you can make it that far?" she goaded.

"Only if I have to."

"You do," she answered. "Besides, Tony's serves the best strawberry cheesecake in town . . . that is, if you like cheese—"

David dropped his arm to Elena's waist, pulling her body close and lowering his mouth to her frozen cheek. "I have always loved good cheesecake," he whispered in a suggestive low growl before planting a featherlight kiss on the rosy spot he had been so coveting for the past ten minutes.

Pulling hastily from his embrace, Elena plunged headlong across the slush-covered street. She hurried on ahead of him through the doorway and picked out a booth on the far side of the room.

She was shaking in the pit of her stomach. She was

disturbed, certainly not because David Atwell had made a physical pass at her, but rather that—even before his lips touched her skin—the familiar teasing sensuality of his voice had unlatched a multitude of latent physical needs she held for him.

She didn't know what he was thinking or expecting, but she would have to put a stop to this immediately. David Atwell had been wrong for her when she was eighteen, but now—now that her career was at stake—she would not let him eat into her concentration. She must keep her thoughts clear. Every physical and emotional gesture must be directed at keeping her job. Nothing must eat into her concentration!

Elena glanced up at Dave's face as he seated himself across from her. His thick brown hair had been blown by the wind and was now as wild and unruly as she had remembered. He smiled, softly and enigmatically. She could not read his expression clearly and was not sure of his thoughts. Yet, she knew. She could feel it in the directness of his soft green eyes as they watched her.

She sensed the leisurely nibbling that had already begun on her block of concentration, as if to David Atwell it were nothing more than a tasty morsel of cheese.

You are a fool to sit here and subject yourself to this, Elena Shubert. You are an utter fool.

Chapter Two

The cafe was a vestige of the fifties, when the world was tiled in pink and gray linoleum. Booths of blond wood and Formica-topped tables displayed numerous gouges and chips from the years of wear and tear. The lighting in the restaurant was provided by bare bulbs hung every six feet across the ceiling, the owners having opted for utility rather than aesthetic appeal.

"I love their decorator," Dave murmured quietly as they seated themselves.

"Do you want good food or elegant decor?" she asked, adding a sarcasm to her remark that she immediately regretted.

Dave merely shrugged indifferently, seemingly oblivious of her tone of voice.

A young, plump waitress, who continuously popped her gum in Dave's face, took their order. The whole time she was writing it on a napkin, she kept an eager eye on the doorway, as if she expected Prince Charming to walk in and rescue her at any minute.

"So," Elena began after they were alone again, "what have you been doing all these years?" She was trying to force into her tone of voice a casualness she did not feel. But it was the only way. *Keep it light, Elena. Light and inconsequential.*

"Playing ball," Dave answered, his hands clasped in front of him on the table and his eyes fixed on

Elena's mouth. It was turning upward into the semblance of a smile. But Dave wasn't fooled. Something was bothering her and she was trying to cover it up.

"Ball?"

"Yes."

"You mean. . . like what. . . like football?"

"Yes, Elena. Remember, I played football in college. I wanted to make the pros. You do remember that, don't you?" Dave didn't know whether to be hurt or angry with her. Could she really remember that little about him, or was she playing some childish game of one-upmanship with him?

"Of course I remember. I just thought maybe you had changed your mind, that's all."

"Oh, I get it." Anger was definitely what he was feeling now. "You thought that I would grow up and decide to do something worthwhile instead of simply tossing a football around, right?"

"David, I didn't mean that," Elena stammered. "I just—"

"What then?" When she didn't answer, Dave turned his head to follow her line of vision. A young boy, about ten or eleven, was moving shyly toward the table at his father's insistence.

"I'm sorry, David," Elena whispered. "I think they want my autograph. I hope you don't mind. It will only take a moment." She smiled at the approaching boy.

"Barnstorming Atwell!" His prepubescent voice cracked with awe. "Are you—are you—"

"Excuse us," the father interrupted. "I'm Jim McIntyre. My son here is a big fan of yours, Mr.

Atwell. And...well, so am I. We...he was wondering if he could get your autograph.''

"You bet.'' Dave smiled, casting a quick glance at Elena's stricken expression. "What's your name, son?''

"Timothy, sir. Wow! The kids at school will never believe it. Wow!''

Dave took a paper napkin and wrote "To Timothy McIntyre, one of my favorite fans. Dave 'Barnstorming' Atwell.'' He handed the paper to the glowing boy. "Do you play football, Tim?''

"Yes, sir,'' he answered with enthusiasm. "I'm— I'm hoping to play for the Cowboys like you.''

"Hey, that's great. But you get yourself a good education first, okay? Study hard, and remember, it's a great way to make a living, but there's more to life than just football.''

"That's what I've been trying to tell him,'' his father said. "Maybe he'll listen to you more than me. We were real sorry about your retirement. We're going to miss seeing you in the league.''

"Thank you, Mr. McIntyre. However, I don't plan on fading away like an old soldier. I'm going to be doing the play by play for some of the televised games this season, so I'll be around.''

"That's great to hear. Thank you for the autograph. Tell Mr. Atwell thank you, Tim.''

"Gee thanks, Mr. Atwell.''

"You're welcome, Tim. Keep practicing...and studying.''

The waitress brought their cheesecake and coffee to the table and Dave turned his attention back to a disconcerted Elena.

"I didn't realize you were a hero," she quipped, her face frozen with embarrassment.

"I'm not a hero, Elena. Far from it. I'm just a football player. Was a football player."

"Yes, but one who is recognized by a ten-year-old kid over a thousand miles away from where you played," she said, frowning.

"That was a fluke. America has kind of adopted the Cowboys as its team in the past few years. All of us players have attained a certain amount of notoriety that we wouldn't have received with any other team."

"I see."

Dave knew she didn't see anything. What was the matter with her anyway? Was she so caught up in her own little world that she couldn't see beyond the end of her nose? Maybe she simply needed a taste of her own medicine.

"And what have you been doing all these years?" he asked, his expression flattened into a poker face.

Elena's head jerked up to stare incredulously at him. "I—I'm a concert pianist," she stated haughtily.

"You mean you do what you did tonight for a living?" He was now having trouble keeping his mouth in a serious line.

"You do remember that that is what I was—" Elena stopped, dumbstruck by the turn the conversation had suddenly taken. He was tossing back the same questions she had thrown at him. She glared reproachfully at David until she noticed the soft twinkling in his eyes. Her mask crumbled and she couldn't stop the smile that lifted the corners of her mouth. "Oh, God, David, I'm sorry."

Dave reached for her hand and stroked the flesh

across her knuckles with his thumb, setting alive nerve endings in her body that were best left alone. "Don't be," he whispered huskily across the table.

She knew she should pull her hand away and suggest that they leave. She should tell him that she didn't want to see him again. But she couldn't.

"Professional football. It's what you wanted, isn't it?" she whispered, even the vocal cords in her throat devastated by his presence.

"It seemed like what I wanted at the time," he said, his hand increasing its pressure on hers.

"You were very good in college." She was looking at him now, seeing him the way he was then. All bone and muscle and lean virility. Young and in love with life. The possibilities had seemed endless to them both. She blinked to force the vision of the past from her mind.

It was with dismay that she noticed David was still all bone and muscle and lean virility. More of a man now than a boy. She wondered if he still had the same enthusiasm for life that he once had.

"You only watched me play in one game," he reminded her with a laugh. "That hardly qualifies you as an expert."

She smiled. "I may not know football, David. But I know a star when I see one, and in that game you were definitely the star."

"Remember how cold it was that day?" He prodded her memory. "I was freezing my tail off down on the field. And I remember once looking up at you in the stands, all snuggled cozily beneath a stadium blanket, your big gray eyes wide with confusion over the game. All I wanted at that moment was to. . ."

His voice trailed off as he gazed directly at Elena's eyes.

He didn't need to go any further, for both of their thoughts had traveled to that same spot in time. That cold, starlit night, so long ago, after the game when they were together alone. Elena remembered every furtive, pleading touch, every urgently whispered word of inexperienced love.

They had shared the warmth of the blanket in the backseat of Dave's car, listening to the sounds of each other's breathing and filling their hearts with a promise that both of them knew could not be kept.

How foolish they had been. Elena shook her head to dispel the memory. She looked at David and his green eyes were burning holes through her expression, reading the thoughts that were beneath the surface.

"We were very young, weren't we?" She tried unsuccessfully to laugh.

"We still are," Dave said.

"Are we?" Elena exhaled a short, disbelieving breath through her nose, and the present crashed in upon them. She pulled her hand away and began picking unenthusiastically at her cake.

Dave was silent for a moment, watching Elena. "That doesn't sound like the girl I knew."

Exasperated, Elena dropped her fork with a clatter to her plate. "I am not the girl you knew, David. Look, we knew each other for one year. We were together a few times. We mistakenly thought, as young people often do, that we were in—in love. We—"

"I've never married, Elena."

Her eyes locked with Dave's and she felt hopelessly encaged in his power.

His eyes narrowed on her in speculation. "I don't think you've ever married either," he decided.

"David, that has nothing to do with you." She cast her eyes downward and once again picked up her fork to make an attempt at her food.

"Then why?" Dave asked, unaware of the untouched cake on his plate and the coffee turning cold in his cup.

"I haven't wanted to. I have been happy with my life the way it is. There is no room, no time, for anyone. I am married to my piano, David. That is my first love."

"That was your excuse at eighteen, Elena. Football was my excuse. I don't believe it anymore...and I don't think you do either."

"You don't know what you're talking about," Elena argued. "In fact, right now my career is more important than it ever has been. I'm at a very critical turning point and—"

"Go on," Dave urged, when a shutter fell across her eyes and she grew silent.

"No, it's nothing." Elena set down her fork and began slipping her arms into her coat. "I really need to be going, David. It was nice—"

"Don't!" Dave demanded, his voice hard and exacting. "Don't say that it was nice seeing me, Elena. Don't pretend that we are nothing more than old college chums."

"David." Elena stood and zipped her fur jacket up to the neck. "If this is some sort of midlife crisis and you are trying to recapture something that may or may not have been, I don't have time for it."

Dave stood and shoved his arms into his jacket,

blocking her path. "Have you ever thought that maybe we were wrong? That maybe we made a mistake walking away from each other?"

"David—"

"No, listen to me." There was an urgency in his voice that wasn't there before. "I haven't thought of us this way before, but I let you convince me that music was your one and only love. I convinced myself that football was my one and only love. But, you see, I'm better able to see mistakes now, Elena. Maybe we were wrong. Dead wrong," he added on a more introspective note.

"You may have been wrong, David," Elena argued, moving toward the door and out into the frigid night air, "but I was not. I have been very... content with my life and have nev—rarely regretted the decisions I made."

"Rarely?" He grasped her arm and spun her around until her body was pressed against his chest. His arms snaked around her waist, holding her next to him. "You said rarely, Elena. I want to know when you regret it."

She struggled in vain to escape his suffocating hold on her body.

"When, Elena?" His voice grated against her ear before being buried beneath the fur collar of her coat. "At night?" he breathed against her throat, sending hot chills across her flesh. "On cold nights when you're lying in bed all alone?"

"What makes you so sure I'm always alone?" she snapped, still struggling unsuccessfully to escape. "What makes you so sure I don't have some ardent lover at home right now waiting for me?" she taunted.

"Oh," he drawled sarcastically, letting her escape his arms. "Is that right? Well, we'll just see about that." He grabbed her firmly by the elbow and pulled her toward the curb, where he began trying to hail a taxi.

"What are you doing?" she asked in alarm.

"We're going to take a taxi to your house and kick your lover—ex-lover—out on his butt."

"David, I was only teasing," Elena cried.

"Sure you were," he replied, undaunted. "I'll just make certain if you don't mind."

"I do mind!" She jerked away from him. "I mind very much. You don't own me, David."

A cab had pulled to the curb, and David opened the back door, disregarding Elena's remark, and patiently waited for her to enter.

"I only live a few blocks from here, David, and I do not need a taxi."

"I do, Elena. I'm freezing."

"Then you ride and I'll walk," she retorted adamantly.

"It's very late at night, and this certainly doesn't look like the safest area of town. I hardly think that your slight frame would be much defense against someone who wished to do you bodily harm."

"Does that include you?" She couldn't help from issuing the snide question.

"Well, I have been a fairly decent running back since I was fourteen years old, and it wouldn't be difficult to catch you. So, I guess that does include me. Now, shall we go?" He tilted his hand toward the waiting cab.

The driver must have had the heater on full blast,

because the air inside the taxi was stifling. After Elena gave the driver brief instructions to her house, they drove past a block of derelict buildings that had been left to ruin because the city didn't have the funds or the social conscience to tear them down.

During the Second World War this part of the city flourished with munitions and armament plants and other industries heavily into the production of war-related materials. But when the tide of peace and complacency swept through the country during the fifties, these factories and foundries were left as casualties of the war years: dark, vacant, and forgotten relics of the past.

And where this row of buildings ended, an old but respectable neighborhood began. In isolated spots where weakened concrete left gaping holes in the road, remains of the original brick street could be seen.

They drove the short distance in silence, Elena repeatedly telling herself that she did not want this man in her life. *Nothing must break into your concentration, Elena. Nothing!*

"It's right here." She pointed to the series of Victorian row houses on the right, relieved that this encounter with David was almost at an end.

When the taxi pulled to the curb, Dave jumped out of his door and, despite his aching leg, made it to her side of the car before she had stepped out.

"Shall I go break every bone in your lover's body?" he threatened softly, wrapping his arms around her waist and pulling her close to him.

Elena flattened her palms on his chest, fully aware that her pulse was racing as fast as his heart was beneath her hand.

"There's no need for that," she answered wistfully.

"I didn't think so. When can I see you again?" His lips touched her ear, warming that side of her face.

"You can't, David. I'm not the girl you once knew. We were like. . . like—"

"Like ships in the night," Dave crooned dramatically.

"Well, I was trying to think of something a little bit more original and eloquent, but yes, that's right." Elena thought carefully before she again spoke. "A moment in time was ours to share, but that moment is gone. Childhood is over, David." As Elena stared up at that steady, square-jawed face, she knew she was lying to herself. It wasn't over. It would never be over. But she also knew that her relationship with this man would have to remain an unfinished symphony, its final chords playing only in her mind.

"You're lying Elena." David peered down at her soft, bewitching face, and as if he had read her mind with uncanny accuracy, he added, "We're like a duet, destined to play different parts and yet incomplete without each other's notes."

Her lips were parted as she listened to him, thinking of the musical notes that might adequately describe the beauty of his eyes. They were undoubtedly his best feature. Their green color was so pale, they shone like near-white beacons in the night sky, their depths as transparent and elusive as Debussyan moonlight. They were like liquid light on a serene moonlit night.

"Good-bye, David." Elena flung herself from his arms, breaking the hypnotic embrace she was in, and bounded up the stoop to her house.

David chuckled lightly as he watched her go. "Good night, Elena," he answered too softly for her to hear. "I think this time I have finally found home."

Elena closed and locked the door behind her, leaning her forehead against the beveled glass panel to still her rapid heartbeat.

Why now? Why did David Atwell have to pick this moment in time to come back into her life? Didn't he realize it was the worst possible moment? He should instinctively know that her lifelong dream of being a concert pianist was starting to crumble around her feet, she thought irrationally. He would have to realize that, if she were to hang on to the fragile threads of her career, every ounce of her concentration must be on the piano.

Lethargically she unzipped her fur coat and slipped it from her arms. She walked slowly to the coat closet and grasped the old-fashioned glass door handle to open it.

A sense of belonging to a different time and place seized her emotions and with it came a longing for days that were no more.

She had lived in this house for over six years and it had served as a tonic to restore equilibrium to two lives.

When Elena's father died seven years ago, he left behind two shattered women, his wife and his daughter. And though Elena never felt close to her mother, the two of them leaned on each other for much-needed support.

To Elena, her father had been the dominant figure

and the driving force in her life. He was the one who had first encouraged her as a toddler when she insisted on banging her fingers on the family piano all afternoon. He was the one who pampered and coddled her, relieving her of any duties around the house so that she could spend her time at the piano. And he was the one who derived so much pleasure from her music.

Elena would have done anything to please her father, and so she worked diligently year after year to improve her skills as a pianist. She had to be perfect...for her father. She could not have lived with herself if she had presented him with anything less.

Mrs. Shubert, on the other hand, had always remained troubled by the cloistered life-style her daughter had adopted. She watched helplessly, year after year, as Elena was pulled deeper and deeper into a world of single-minded devotion to her music. She worried that Elena had so few girl friends, distressed even more that her daughter didn't seem to care.

But, as she had from the beginning, she stayed in the background of her daughter's life, loving her and feeling sorry for her at the same time.

When her husband died, she was left a bereft widow, mourning the loss of a loving twenty-three-year marriage. But she began to worry more about her daughter than herself, for Elena's grief had pushed her farther into the world she and her father had shared for so many years.

Devastated by the loss of her father, Elena turned more and more to her piano for comfort and escape. Her music became the link to him, and she was driven to play so that she could still somehow please him.

So Mrs. Shubert moved in with Elena and continued her well-practiced role as caretaker. Elena had only to play the piano. Her mother made the meals, cleaned the house, washed the clothes, and drove Elena wherever she needed to go.

Five months ago Elena's mother had remarried and moved to California. Now Elena was forced to make the necessary adjustments of taking care of the house and her life on her own. She had stopped thinking of her mother's remarriage as a defection, realizing that she deserved a life of her own. And too Elena supposed it was high time she learned to do a few things for herself.

Closing the closet door on her memories, she turned to the living room for reassurance from her familiar surroundings. Next to her music she loved this old house more than anything.

It had been built in 1910 and every appointment and detail had been lovingly crafted. The floors were hardwood, polished to a deep molasses-colored glow, and the previous owner had transformed the interior to create a spacious feeling of openness. One wall of the living room, furnished in an assortment of antiques and trailing green plants, had been windowed from floor to ceiling to overlook the garden in back. On the far wall was a narrow stairway that led to the sleeping loft above. A tiny kitchen with ceramic tile counter tops and a butcher block table were off to the left of the living room. With only two bedrooms, it was not a large house, but she was comfortable with its old world charm.

She walked over to her most cherished posses-sion—a vintage Steinway grand that she had salvaged four years ago from the ruins of an old playhouse that was nearly destroyed by a fire. The piano had been in the playhouse for years, producing immortal melodies for every type of theatrical performance, from vaudeville to Bob Fosse.

She ran her hand across the gleaming pecan finish, the one she had so lovingly stripped of its multiple layers of old varnish. She thought of the long days she and her best friend, Marilee, had spent restaining and oiling and tuning it to perfection. It became an entity with whom she spent hours upon hours com-muning, speaking with her well-trained fingers and being answered by richly harmonic refrains.

She sat down on the bench that she had covered with a crewel pad, and her right thumb slid down the keys in an effortless glissando. Her left hand lifted to the keyboard and she began playing a Chopin noc-turne. Her fingers tripped sweetly and slowly over the keys, moving in perfect andantino tempo, swelling through the crescendo passages, prolonging the notes at precisely the measure where sostenuto was called for—

Her hands slammed to the keyboard and her head dropped in dejection over them. Of all the men she should run into! David Atwell! Why couldn't it have been someone who meant nothing to her, someone who could glide into her conscious mind and flow right on through without clutching the very marrow of her bones?

She lifted herself dejectedly from the bench and, after turning out the numerous antique lamps, each glowing circle of light folding into a darkness that matched her mood, she climbed the stairway to the loft, utter fatigue filling every cavity of her body.

After turning on the hot water tap in the bathtub, Elena slipped out of her black dress. For performances she wore more makeup than usual, so it took extra time removing its traces. She poured into the tub some fragrant oils that smelled like honeysuckle, then eased her tired body into the warm water.

Look at it logically, Elena, she instructed herself. Maybe she was making more out of David's remarks than had been intended. By tomorrow he probably would have forgotten all about her and she wouldn't even hear from him again.

Sighing, she knew she was deluding herself. David had meant exactly what he said. And she didn't for the life of her know what she was going to do about him.

Maybe she should ask Marilee. She always knew how to handle men. But no, Marilee would probably insist, as she continually did, that Elena needed a man. She could already hear her friend's earthy advice. "It's positively unhealthy, Elena!" she would say. "You should go out, grab the first half-decent man you can find, and lock yourself up in a room with him for a week."

Elena shook the voice from her mind, leaving only the weariness behind. She climbed from the tub and dried herself with a large Turkish towel, then dusted her body with powder and slipped into an old-fashioned cream-colored cotton gown that hung to her ankles. It had long sleeves that ruffled at the wrists and smocking across the front and back of the bodice that was beaded through with blue satin ribbon.

She unbraided the two coils that held her thick, waist-length hair away from her face and brushed through the whorling strands at least fifty times in an unsuccessful effort to reduce the stubborn curls.

Finally she crawled between the clean sheets on her brass bed, knowing that sleep would be the only thing that could renew her spirit. Pulling the antique quilt up to her chin, she snuggled deeper against her lace-trimmed pillow.

Her mind began to drift through various languorous, somnolent melodies in an effort to lull herself to sleep. But sleep would not come.

The impressionistic sounds and tonal colors of Debussy's "Clair de Lune" began to play through her head, and the vision of a moonlit night so long ago drifted before her eyes....

It had been a cold winter night in Missouri, the first heavy snowfall of the year dropping large crystal flakes onto the ground around David's car. She had half-reclined in the backseat, her back resting against David's chest, his strong arms circling her body from behind. She had been listening to the steady beat of his heart becoming more and more irregular as the minutes rolled on.

His hands, under her sweater, moved slowly and delicately across her stomach, worshiping touches against her sensitive skin. Her head dropped back on his shoulder, her mind relishing the glorious sensations he created inside of her.

She had shifted sideways, joining their bodies more intimately in the confines of the car. The stadium blanket was pulled from the floorboard and draped across her side, and she nestled her head under his chin.

His hands began their magic once more under her sweater, climbing higher to unclasp her bra and spread his trembling fingers across the gentle rise of her breasts.

His mouth trailed soft kisses across her temple and cheek until it reached her lips, where his own became more insistent and fervent, his moist tongue reaching into her mouth to draw the fresh passion from her—

Elena bolted upright in her bed, her breath tremulous and rasping, her palms damp with perspiration. No! She would not let him do this to her. She would not! There was too much at stake to let him or anyone else force their way into her realm of concentration. She must intensify her focus on her career!

"No child prodigy is going to move me out of my position with this symphony," she whispered aloud defiantly. *And, you, David Atwell, are not going to make me think that we are meant as a duet. I am a soloist. I have been a soloist since the day I said good-bye to you twelve years ago, and I will continue to remain one long after you have abandoned any attempts to woo me with your sensuous night music.*

Chapter Three

Time played an endless song of yearning throughout the night, making it impossible for Elena to rest adequately. But, even though she had been blessed with only a few transient moments of dreamless sleep, she was out of bed at seven o'clock, had eaten one piece of toast, and was drinking her hot tea while she sat at the piano.

Since she was six years old, she had always led a disciplined life, centered around piano. Even when she was a young child, her father and her teacher had both expected her to practice four hours daily on her piano lessons. In college those daily practice sessions had extended to six hours.

After college she studied with one of the best teachers her parents' hard-earned money could buy, entering as many competitions around the country as she could. She qualified for some of the best, yet never finished first in any of them. She was a good pianist, she knew. But the competition in the field was fierce and there always seemed to be someone who had that little extra bit of style that enabled him or her to surpass Elena in the final judging.

By the age of twenty-five most pianists were established in their careers. They had either been hired for various city symphony orchestras or else they had resigned themselves to a career in teaching.

Marilee Hennesy was one of those who had accepted such a fate. She and Elena had met at the studio of their piano teacher. Though Marilee had inherited a pure strain of genes and blue blood, in personality she was more like a hybrid whose seeds had been blown through the wind, landing indiscriminately in her family's cultivated garden.

It was her family's belief that musical training was an integral part of a young lady's breeding. But as Marilee was fond of saying, "There's another gem to add to the compost heap." Not in the least interested in what a proper young lady should do, Marilee had fun.

Whatever triggered Elena and Marilee to seek each other out as friends was a mystery to both. Perhaps it was that both detected in the other the missing elements of their own personalities. Elena held the serious nature that Marilee was without. And Marilee represented the freedom and frivolous exuberance of life that Elena had never known.

Although Marilee finally settled down at twenty-five into a career of music education, teaching third and fourth grade in an expensive private school, her life existed in the social sphere after hours.

Elena realized that a philosophy of life such as Marilee's could never work for her. Her life was her work, and her work, her life. Without that she was nothing.

Though Elena was now thirty and had been lucky enough to be chosen at the age of twenty-two from the many applicants for this position with the orchestra, she still dreamed of becoming one of the great pianists of her generation.

Every morning after breakfast she spent four hours at the piano, practicing concerto after concerto, working with various interpretations of a composer's work. At noon she would stop for a short lunch break, then spend the afternoon in rehearsal with the rest of the orchestra.

If there was not to be a performance at night, she would again sit at her piano after dinner, creating and synthesizing her own compositions for hours on end. It was the life she had known for the eight years she had been with the orchestra. The beat of her heart and the very breath of her soul were centered on this one thing, this one aim, this one note.

It was particularly annoying when this day did not follow that same routine.

It was around ten o'clock when she received the telephone call. She was in the middle of a Saint-Saëns concerto when Alexi called and destroyed her systematic routine.

"Hello, my turtle dove," he began with his usual effete insincerity. "Just thought you'd like to know that Little Miss Blue Eyes is going to be playing this morning for our illustrious directors. I'm sure you wouldn't want to miss such a dazzling performance. Elena? Are you there, Elena?"

"I'm here," she answered sullenly.

"Well, I won't keep you from your toil, my love. Just wanted to cheer you up a bit."

"You're a real bastard, Alexi."

"Oh, aren't we feeling testy this morning. Well, ten thirty is when she begins. *Au revoir, mon petit chou.*"

Elena grasped the receiver tightly in her fingers

when she heard Alexi hang up. As she replaced the phone onto its cradle, her hands were shaking. She had seen this moment coming for several weeks now. But to actually have it at hand was almost too much to bear.

Tina Volkowski, the nineteen-year-old niece of one of the directors of the symphony organization, was considered a child prodigy when she entered the Julliard School of Music at the age of seven. Then, because of a freak accident that broke her left hand in three places, she was set back in her quest to become a world-renowned pianist.

However, after several years of intensive rehabilitation and retraining, little Tina was ready to take on the world once again.

Tina was supposed to be a very good pianist, and yet Elena wondered if, without the influence of her aunt, Tina would have gotten even this far. Still, would the directors go so far as to replace Elena with a mere child?

When she had questioned Alexi about it before, he had merely shrugged his shoulders noncommittally. But the rumors had been flying during the past few weeks, and Elena had felt undue pressure at every performance. She knew she was being watched—closely. She knew she was constantly being compared to this fresh young talent.

This was her life, dammit! If she were to lose this job, there would be nowhere for her to go. No well-respected orchestra would hire a has-been who was over thirty years old. Today symphony orchestras wanted their performers fresh out of the egg or not at all.

Elena sat back down at the piano, refusing to let Alexi's call interrupt her routine. She had no intention of going to the hall to hear Tina play. Why should she subject herself to that kind of torture?

She played through a few more pages of the concerto, her fingers faltering several times before she closed the book with a sigh. She would go. Alexi had known that she would and he would no doubt get some sort of sadistic delight in watching Elena squirm.

Slipping out of her brushed denim jeans and smock top, she dressed in a paisley dirndl skirt, blue cowl-neck sweater, and brown suede boots. She kept telling herself over and over that she did not need to go to so much trouble, but even as she chided herself, she continued to apply just the right amount of makeup, braid her hair into two sections, then wrap them in a chignon at the back of her head.

Her hand automatically reached for the bottle of perfume that contained the fragrance she always wore.

When she was a young girl, she would practice the piano hour upon long hour by an open window in the living room. Outside the window honeysuckle vines grew wild and abundant along the fence. The sweet scent of those delicate flowers wafted through the open window, touching Elena's subconscious with the notion of what it must be like to grow free and wild.

Wearing that honeysuckle fragrance always gave her a sense of unbridled freedom that she could find nowhere else.

As she walked to the auditorium, engulfed in her

long blue cape to insulate her from the cold, gray day, she had the chance to put this all into perspective. After all, the girl had a right to try out for the position. And the other directors must have felt obligated to listen to the niece of one of their own members. Of course, that's all it was. An obligation. Alexi had been tormenting Elena for his own twisted delight, not because he believed for one minute that this girl could possibly take over Elena's spot.

The closer she came to the concert hall, the more relaxed and buoyant her stride became. She looked around her at the gray winter pallor and intuitively sensed the coming of blue skies and brighter days.

As with the impermanence of spring, Elena's ebullient feelings were short-lived.

Her face was growing paler by the minute as she listened to Tina Volkowski play. The auditorium was empty, except for the directors who sat like a firing squad in the front row. Elena had taken a seat in the back row where she hoped she could remain inconspicuous.

Tina was playing Beethoven's Fifth, and the more Elena listened, the more worried she became. The walls of the auditorium seemed to shudder with the rich tones coming from the piano.

The girl was like a fragile, moon-faced doll, Elena acknowledged with a sick feeling. There was no doubt about that. And, because she made a habit of dressing like she was fifteen, she projected an even more touchingly sweet image on stage.

As she listened to the climax of the piece, Elena closed her eyes and admitted for the first time that the end might be at hand. The realization was an incredible blow to her pride.

This spot with the orchestra was what she had worked for all her life. She had never found the time to develop friendships with more than a few people. She had missed out on many youthful activities because she had to practice. In college she practiced the piano for so many hours that she was too tired to pursue a social life. She worked every day at improving her skills as a pianist. It wasn't fair that someone else could come along and take this away from her. She had too many years invested to give it all up now.

Before the final chord of the symphony was struck, Elena quietly slipped out of the auditorium and walked dejectedly down the wide stone steps.

Suddenly winter was back upon her with full force, and as she sat down on a bench across the sidewalk from the building, she stared gloomily at nothing.

The world she had known was collapsing beneath her. But why? And how? How could a young girl who did not have the benefit of Elena's years of experience possibly have more to offer to the symphony?

She couldn't imagine what on earth she was going to do with her own life. This was all she had ever known. All she had ever wanted to be.

Marilee couldn't understand that. Elena's mother couldn't understand that. And if David meant what he said last night about the two of them, then he did not understand it either. Why was it so difficult for everyone to accept that this was her life?

Her face was drawn into harrowed lines and her eyes looked pale and listless against the lead-colored sky. Her thoughts, though rebellious and reproachful, moved through the grooves of her mind in a slow, laborious cadence.

The minutes dragged by as she reflected moodily on her grim situation. She was even more dismayed as she watched a figure moving toward her and realized it was David. She didn't want to see him. She didn't want him to see her this way. It was the wrong time for him to come back into her life!

As he sat down beside her on the cold concrete bench, she looked up into pale green eyes that were washed gray to match the winter sky and into a steady and controlled face that contrasted sharply with her own self-analysis.

"Hi." Dave's voice held a remnant of youthful expectancy.

"Don't you have work to do?" she asked unkindly, wanting him to go away and leave her alone.

"Yes. But I've learned that all work and no play makes Dave a very dull boy. And what about you? Why aren't you in there tickling the ivories?"

She looked away, trying to stop the tears from overflowing her lower eyelids. *Don't think about it. Don't talk about it. If you talk about it, then you are admitting the possibility that it could happen. Keep reminding yourself, this is only a slight setback in your career. You will overcome this obstacle, this competitive upstart. You must not let this get to you.... Damn!*

"It's a good thing there are fallback positions for a football player," she mused, not noticing the tightening of David's jaw as she said this.

"Fallback positions?" He smirked. "You've got to be kidding."

She looked at him, not seeing the hidden emotions beyond the surface of his controlled expression. "Well, you seemed to have found an easy transition anyway," she added, a tinge of envy adding a petulant tone to her voice.

"It's never easy to give up something that means so much to you." He turned toward her with a quizzical look. Is that what was bothering her? Maybe she was worried about what she was going to do when she no longer played concert piano. He opened his mouth, starting to ask her, but the closed expression on her face did not invite personal questions, so he pressed his lips together, holding the thoughts inside.

"Are these the people you play with?" he asked instead as he watched the constant stream of musicians filing into the music hall.

"Some of them," she answered agreeably, relieved that he had tactfully changed the subject. "Some must be students here for a competition."

"Ah, that must be Tweedledum and Tweedledee." Elena followed his gaze to the pair of short, stout men who were carrying their cello cases into the building.

"Well, you're close." Elena couldn't help but smile. "They do live together. Quite cozily, I might add, but there is a third."

"Oh, a ménage à trois. That is cozy. Who is that one?" He was now watching a thin, dour matron, dressed in a plain black coat with a frayed hem that was dragging the ground.

"That's Elizabeth Cornbly, second violinist," Elena answered with an involuntary smile.

"With that bubbly expression, she must have been the model for Grant Wood's *American Gothic.*"

Despite her unreleased feelings of depression, Elena could not suppress a giggle. David had always been able to do that to her. Even in college, no matter how dispirited she was over her endless studies of music theory, or when she was nervous over an upcoming recital, he would always find the way to lift her spirits.

She looked at him closely, her eyes softening with the memories. He really had been her best friend.

"And what have we here?" he drawled lazily, pulling her mind back from the past.

"That's Henri Beaumont, flute," Elena explained. "His name is really Henry, but he becomes absolutely livid if anyone calls him that."

"We should go peek in his windows some night," David whispered conspiratorily to Elena. "What do you want to bet he practices his flute in the nude? Except for the gold chains around his neck, of course."

"You're probably right." Elena laughed.

David began chuckling and she turned to see what had caught his attention. She too laughed at the pear-shaped man who was walking down the sidewalk, carrying a coronet case.

"Don't tell me." David laughed. "On his days off he doubles as a pin at the local bowling alley, right?"

"How could you tell?" She grinned at him. "Now, that is our resident hippie." She pointed to the person who traversed the packed mounds of snow on roller skates. Dressed in army fatigues and moccasins, with hair hanging past the shoulder blades, the musician looked like a lost orphan.

"She's real cute," David replied facetiously.

"She happens to be a he," Elena informed him.

David shook his head slowly. "I don't think I can take any more of this. Besides, aren't you ashamed of yourself, talking about your fellow musicians this way?" he scolded.

"Me!" Elena's expression was indignant. "You started it." She glanced down at David's hand where it was massaging his right thigh. "What's the matter with your leg?"

He pulled his hand back quickly. He had been unaware that he was rubbing it. "It gets a little stiff in the cold air, that's all. I need to exercise it. Will you walk with me?"

Slamming a shutter closed against the past, Elena reverted immediately back to her state of depression and shook her head. She had to go home and practice. She should not have been wasting this time with David in the first place. Why had he come here? What on earth did he want from her? She had to keep her mind on track. Tina was in there, playing her rotten little heart out, and Elena knew that the next two or three performances were going to be crucial. She would have to practice extra hard. She would have to prepare her mind and body for this as yet unofficial competition.

"No, David," she answered emphatically, her chin tilted at an assertive angle. "I have to practice."

"Look, I didn't come all the way over here this morning and use up some of my best one-liners just to have you reject me. I must tell you, Elena, I don't take rejection very well." He was smiling, and despite her good intentions, she felt herself slipping into the steady stream of his easy charm.

But she continued to shake her head, trying to answer him and dispel his power over her at the same time.

"Besides—" he grasped her upper arms, turning her so that he could see her face better "—I want to know what it is that caused you to look like a crushed flower. When I walked up a while ago, I expected to hear you singing a funeral dirge."

"I was just thinking." Elena tried to keep a tone of annoyance in her voice, but something about the way he had described her made her eyes sparkle.

"That's better." He smiled down into her flower-like face. "Now you look like a spring blossom that perhaps only needs some food and drink and a little tender loving care."

"David," she sighed in weary frustration. "You don't know what you're saying. This can't go anywhere, don't you know that? I cannot simply pick up where we left off. My life is in enough turmoil right now. I do not have time for a relationship."

Dave's arms slipped through the large side openings of her cape, wrapping around her waist.

"David, don't...please."

Dave watched the pulse that fluttered spontaneously in the side of her throat and he smiled. "You don't mean that, Elena."

"I don't have time," she cried. "I just don't have—"

Dave's mouth closed over hers in midsentence, forcing any more excuses she might have had back down her throat, and his hands began clutching her sides with an intensity that almost terminated permanently the beating of her heart.

His mouth was warm and moist over hers, his tongue once again searching the velvet softness of her inner mouth. She was swept into the majesty of his embrace, the sumptuous taste and feel of his mouth sending reckless waves of abandon through her mind and body, dragging any sensible, pragmatic thoughts out to sea.

When he pulled away to look at her face, her eyes were closed the way they had been on that other January night so long ago. She had accused him of wanting to pick up where they had left off twelve years ago. But that wasn't what he wanted at all. Too much had happened for them to ever recapture what they once were. Yet he had known when he saw her last night, for the first time since college, that there was a strain of music that ran between them, a ballad of tones and patterns that was in them both. All it needed was the right touch, the right mood, and it could become a masterpiece, a rhapsody of passion.

Elena's gray Alice in Wonderland eyes opened wide to stare in confusion at his arresting face. What was happening to her? He was moving with unrelenting determination into her life and she couldn't seem to stop him!

Her mouth parted with a new excuse, but before she could utter a word, David put a finger across her lips to silence her, smiling gently. "Let's go get some lunch," he suggested.

"I have to practice, David." She tried again to

sound assertive, but her voice held little conviction.

"Look, you have to eat. Just a quick lunch and then I promise I'll let you practice."

She sighed reluctantly. "All right. I suppose I do have to eat." Elena frowned at her own hopeless inability to project the image of coolness she wanted.

Dave shook his head in amused exasperation. He had hoped for a little more enthusiasm, but then perhaps he was expecting too much, too soon.

"There's a deli close by that I saw on the way over here." He wrapped his arm protectively around her shoulders and began leading her to his car.

She stopped, glancing quizzically at his leg. "You're limping, David. And I noticed that you were last night too."

"I'm afraid that's permanent." He scowled briefly before shrugging away the problem. "Too many defensive linemen tried to tear it off me."

"You broke it?"

He chuckled at her naiveté. "No, it was more like it was twisted into the shape of a pretzel."

"Is that why you quit?"

They had reached his dark blue Mercedes and he propped his body against the hood, taking most of the weight off his sore leg. He was looking beyond her in the direction of the music hall. "I guess I reached the end of a stage in my life."

"That's all football was you to, a stage?"

David turned his face toward Elena and frowned. He had thought it was much more than that, and yet he had been so wrong.

"That's all it was," he answered with finality, moving from the car and opening the driver's door.

"Listen, would you do me a favor and drive? My leg is a little stiff in this cold weather."

"Drive!" Elena cast a startled look at Dave.

He stared back at her, incredulous. "Do you mean to tell me, Elena Shubert, that you still have not learned to drive?"

"I took driver's training a few years ago, but I never found the time to get my license." She scowled at the apologetic sounds that were coming from her own mouth. Until recently her mother had driven her wherever she wanted to go. She had nothing to be ashamed of. She lived so close to the music hall that she could walk. If she needed to go anywhere else, she always took a taxi.

"A thirty-year-old woman who doesn't know how to drive!" He was shaking his head in amusement.

"I have no need to drive," she defended herself. "I can walk to the music hall from my house. There is no reason for me to have a car."

"But what about when you're no longer playing with the symphony? Won't you—"

"I will always play with the symphony!" she exploded, causing Dave to jump with surprise. "I am a concert pianist and I have no intention of becoming anything else."

His gaze narrowed on her, reading the lines around her pinched mouth, the fire in her blazing eyes. She was scared! But what in the hell was she afraid of? Something must be happening in her career to cause her to react this way. He could ask her, but as jumpy as she was, she probably wouldn't give him a straight answer. Well, he would wait. *Let her tell you in her own time,* he instructed himself. There was a more immediate problem at hand.

He placed a possessive hand on the car, while he ran some possibilities through his mind. His new Mercedes with its beautiful, expensive paint job! Did he dare? "Get in," he commanded with a slight hesitation. "You're going to get a driving lesson."

"David, I don't—"

He interrupted her denial by pointing decisively at her and then at the car. She entered on the driver's side, but only after her irritable sigh reached his ears. She failed to see the amused smile that lifted the corners of his mouth.

"Now," he began after they were lashed to the seat with their safety belts. "Start the engine. Turn the key to the right, Elena."

The motor ground and screamed as if it were being tortured.

"For God's sake, it's started, Elena, it's started!" He cringed at the thought of what she was doing to the finely tuned engine.

She took her hand off the key and turned a hurt face toward him. "Look, if you're going to yell at me the whole way, you can just drive yourself."

"Okay, I'm sorry." He patted her arm in appeasement. "Patience was never my strong suit." He took a deep breath. "Now, let's begin again. The first thing to remember is to glance often in your rearview mirror and drive defensively. You never know what some of those maniacs out there are going to do."

"David, I think I've changed my mind. I don't want to learn to drive."

"You're not going to get out of this, Elena."

"But maniacs!"

"Look, relax. You'll fit right in with them."

"Thanks a lot."

"Now, put the car into drive and pull away slowly from the curb."

"Drive?"

Dave expelled a slow breath, trying very hard not to show his impatience. Maybe this wasn't such a good idea, after all.

"I thought you said you took driver training," he mumbled.

"I did," she answered defensively. "But it was ten years ago."

"Okay," he sighed, wiping the sweat from his palms. "See this letter D? That stands for drive. Pull the gear shift down to the D. No, that's N for neutral. That's it. Now slowly put your foot on the gas."

The car lurched violently into the street, accompanied by Elena's gasp and Dave's horrified, ashen expression.

"The brake, Elena! Put your foot on the brake!"

Flung toward the dashboard, the two occupants were saved from concussions only by the strength of their seat belts.

"I never thought I'd say it," Dave mumbled under his breath. "But thank God for Ralph Nader."

The drive to the delicatessen, which in actuality was only a few blocks away, seemed an endless journey. The car moved in spasms and spurts toward its destination, each of its occupants becoming more distraught with each bucking inch.

"This has got to be worse than Mr. Toad's wild

ride!'' Dave complained at one point, only to be severely censured by Elena's stricken expression.

Though neither verbally expressed their relief at arriving at the store, it was plainly evident in their long, loosening sighs.

''Serves you right for being so damned insistent, David Atwell,'' Elena grumbled under her breath as they both climbed out of the car.

Standing at the counter in the small ready-to-eat store, Elena gawked in amazement as David ordered a huge carton of potato salad, mounds of smoked ham, a fat kielbasa sausage, and a half pound of sliced pepper cheese.

''That ordeal made me hungry,'' he offered as an excuse.

Elena's tight-lipped smile was stoical as she tried to ignore the inference.

When they returned to the car, Dave quickly opened the passenger door for Elena. ''My leg feels much better now.''

Elena knew that was a lie. She watched him limping slightly as he walked out of the store and to the driver's side.

''Do you mind if we eat this at your house?'' he asked while driving in precisely that direction. ''I'm still in a hotel until I find a place to live.''

Elena held her hands tightly clasped around the bag of food, hoping that David couldn't see or hear the paper sack rattle as her fingers shook. She didn't want him in her house. That would mean he was getting too close to her, becoming too much a part of her life, squeezing into her self-reliant world.

Dave glanced at her for her answer and, hearing

none, assumed that she was agreeable to that arrangement. Pulling alongside the curb in front of her building, he parked the car and helped her out, and reluctantly Elena led him into her fortress of solitude.

Dave's eyes traveled with mixed emotions around every square inch of Elena's house, absorbing the antique flavor and whimsical charm of the decor, but sensing that there was something unreal and cloistered about it that could become suffocating. Plants hung everywhere! Ferns and ivy and trailing spider plants. On shelves and end tables were African violets and prayer plants. The only patch of light in the gray sky was shining through the tall windows on the back wall.

Dave looked at Elena busily laying out the food on the butcher block table, her hands fluttering away at any task she could find to avoid him. She might argue that she was not the same person she had been at eighteen, but she was. Twelve years had perhaps etched a little more determination in those fine lines around her eyes, but she was still that same idealist who truly believed that she could wrap herself in a dream, isolated from the drowning reality of human voices.

He had been there too, but no longer. He had stubbornly believed that his football career was all he would ever need, that he somehow existed in a plane outside normal existence. But he had found out the hard way that his reach had far exceeded his grasp and only now was he learning to live in the real world.

He looked around him again at the domain Elena

had created for herself. A world in the past, a world of perennial green life, a world of endless music. A closed world.

She was standing in the doorway of the kitchen now, her gray eyes watching him as he watched her. He wanted to reach out and touch her, lift her into his arms and keep her protected forever from the harsh realities of life. She had lived in this world for so long. Perhaps he didn't have the right to ask her to enter his.

They ate their lunch in relative silence, she feeling ill at ease, he not sure what he was feeling. He had lived alone for so many years, relatively content with his life. There had never been room for anyone on a permanent basis. Football had been his life. Every breath, every gesture, every ounce of feeling had been directed toward that one goal.

He had not taken the time or energy to look for any other meaningful aspect to his life. Football was it. It had given him a sense of purpose, a sense of direction.

His college degree had been in a field that did not prepare one for any substantial professional career. He had banked on being a football player. That was to be his life. He was going to build his future around it.

He had been a damned fool.

He looked across the table at Elena and wished that he could, for one moment, be endowed with the hand of God, able to turn back the clock to that moment in time when they came to a crossroads and said good-bye. If he could go back, perhaps he could see it all more clearly. He could evaluate it and find the reasons for it.

"Why did you leave Missouri, Elena?" He leaned his forearms on the table, his eyes centered on the now tight line of her mouth. The question had to be asked. He had to at least make an attempt to understand it.

Elena was picking with her fork at the potato salad on her plate, rearranging the untouched food into neat little piles. She did not want to answer. She did not want to think about the choices she had made in her life and about whether they had been the right ones.

"I remember the reason you gave me at the time," Dave continued when she didn't answer. "You said it was because you could get a better classical foundation elsewhere."

"That's right," she answered without looking up. She couldn't look at him. David Atwell knew her too well. He would see the lie in the depths of her eyes.

He wrapped his fingers around her hand, feeling the heat that automatically surged through her flesh. "I'm going to ask you again," he spoke softly. "Why, Elena? Why did you leave Missouri...leave me?"

She finally looked up and her eyes were brimming with moisture. "You're being very unfair, David. It was you as much as me. You had your future all mapped out for yourself. I didn't fit into your life. You didn't fit into mine."

She brusquely pulled her hand away from his fingers' embrace. "Why can't you accept what was and what is? Just because two people had a relationship

at one point in their lives does not mean it has to
resume twelve years later. You have to realize—''

''You're right,'' he interrupted. ''It can't resume...if it never ended.''

''I don't believe you!'' Elena cried, jumping up
from the table and carrying her plate to the sink,
where she dumped her untouched food unceremoni-
ously down the disposal. She turned back to him with
an exasperated look. ''Are you trying to tell me that
you've been pining away all these years for me? That
you've been waiting to pick up where we left off
twelve years ago?''

Dave pushed back from the table and walked over
to the counter where she was standing with her back
to the edge. He leaned close, placing his hands on the
counter to each side of her body. Tilting her head
back to look up at him, she was startled by the close-
ness of his face to her own. She was waiting for his
answer, hoping it would be the one she had been trying to deny.

''No, Elena. I have not been pining away for
you.'' His eyes traveled across her face, across
features that hid any disappointment she might have
felt. ''I rarely even thought about you.'' He smiled as
he watched her features finally crumble into a more
normal human response.

''Well, good,'' she blurted in retaliation. ''Then
the problem is settled. I haven't thought about you
either. I have been very happy with my life and, con-
trary to what most men might like to believe, I do not
need a man to define the parameters of my existence.
And—''

Her voice trailed off in a lost chord as David's lips

touched her forehead. His mouth moved dolcissimo across her hairline, soft, sweet kisses that stimulated the nerves beneath the surface of her flesh. In playful scherzando his lips dipped down to a spot on her neck, sending tremulant vibrations of want and desire through every neuron of her body.

Without willful intent Elena turned her head to bring his mouth in line with hers. Needing no further invitation, David's lips conjoined with hers in a stirring serenade that awakened the fibers of need that had lain dormant in both of them for so long.

His hands lifted to unclasp the braids at the back of her hair, his fingers unwinding the thick, russet waves as they fell down her back.

He pulled her body away from the counter and into his embrace, his hands pressing against her hips as he held her close.

Her fists had been clenched at her sides in an attempt to thwart this assault on her hidden desires. But now she let her hands rise naturally to his arms, gliding slowly upward to drape around his neck. The feelings that he invoked in her! The memories! The needs!

She clutched the back of his neck as his tongue began to taste the interior of her mouth. Her own began to respond, and they touched and rolled and played together in the warm, moist depths.

Moving his hands across her back, he kept her tightly against him, urgently pulling her into the warmth of his body.

Her heart was palpitating like a metronome at staccato beat, and she could feel the same agitation beneath his rib cage. She let her fingers play across the strength of his neck and shoulders, grabbing the muscles that contracted beneath her hands.

Had she really ever forgotten what his body felt like next to hers? Had she ever let go of the need that only he seemed able to set aflame?

His mouth trailed away from hers, and she felt his breath so warm and ragged against her ear.

"Elena," he whispered urgently. "I lied. I've never stopped thinking about you. I've never felt the same powerful...the same need...God." He pulled his head back to look down at her, the back of his hand brushing softly across her cheek. "As much as I talk, you'd think I'd be better at expressing my feelings, but then I think you know what it is you do to me, don't you?"

Liquid fire was in her eyes as she gazed upward at the strong, arresting features that were dominating her soul. She knew. For to her, the thrill of touching him was as mystical and noble as the vibrating strains of a Bach mass.

She reached up to touch his cheek in affirmation when the sudden shrill ring of the phone shattered the sensitive threads of fantasy that had been woven in the air around them.

"Yes!" she rasped hoarsely into the phone. "Hello."

"What in the hell do you think you're doing?" Alexi shrieked through the phone wires.

Elena turned startled eyes toward the back window, wondering for one split second if Alexi had perhaps been spying on the two of them. "What—what do you mean?"

"I mean, my little precious, that I have a schedule

to keep. We had an open rehearsal programmed for noon today and I expect my musicians to be on time or at least to have a damned good excuse. Now, what is yours?'' he demanded.

Oh, God. Noon rehearsal. And an open rehearsal for the public at that! What time was it? How could she have forgotten a rehearsal? She had never ever been so irresponsible.

She glared at David. It was his fault. He was doing this to her. *Get him out of your life, Elena. He is wrecking what little chance you have left with this orchestra.*

The one person she absolutely must not upset was Alexi. His voice carried too much weight with the directors. If he was angry with her, he might decide to encourage Tina Volkowski, supporting her before the symphony board.

Damn you, David Atwell. He had almost taken her career from her when she was eighteen. And now he seemed bent on the same goal. She did not have time for him.

If he insisted on coming around, she would have to put on blinders whenever he was near. Her position with the symphony meant too much to her to let anyone interfere. Without that, she was nothing.

''I'll be there in five minutes, Alexi,'' she cried apologetically.

''Make it three,'' he commanded.

Chapter Four

"Shut up!" she snapped at the fluorescent lights that buzzed above her head in the practice room, then began repeating the last four bars of the piece she was working on. Her fingers tripped up in the same measure that had been giving her so much trouble all morning. This passage continuously eluded her. Why couldn't she get the damn tempo right?

Sighing, she tried it again, this time with a slight improvement. She moved on through the piece, but her fingers faltered in several different places.

She was trying hard not to let the threat of Tina Volkowski paralyze her with fear. Elena had talent. She had experience. Surely she had more to offer the symphony than Tina.

She yelled at the lights again, this time for blinking off and on, and continued to plod through the music.

She was at least grateful that she had been able to avoid David all week. He had called her a couple of times, but she had always been heading out the door and hadn't had time to talk. She had been practicing more and more at the music hall in the practice rooms that were available. She had to stay away from him or she might find herself in even more trouble than she was already in. Alexi was still bent out of shape over her tardiness for practice the other day. She mustn't do anything else to turn him against her.

She was going to need him in her fight against Tina Volkowski.

Elena set up the metronome on the lid of the piano and adjusted it for the correct beats per measure. Beginning again, she tried to sustain the tempo through the more difficult passages. Again and again she went over the notes, counting out loud, working her fingers until the muscles in her hands and wrists ached from sustaining the tension.

Finally, in exasperation, she closed the sheet music, put away her metronome and, with one final curse at the humming lights, she walked out of the music room, nodded hello to a colleague in the hallway, then left the concert hall for home.

Turning the key in her door, she felt a sense of peace and security once more. As she entered the calm, quiet sanctity of her home, she was aware of the tension ebbing away.

In her kitchen she flipped on the overhead fluorescent light, relieved that she did not hear a single buzz. She pulled a can of potato soup from the cupboard, emptied it into a saucepan, and heated it over the stove. After finding some crackers in her near-empty cupboard, she lined them up evenly on her plate next to the soup bowl, then fixed a cup of hot tea and sat at the table by the window to eat.

The sun had finally found a path through the thick layer of clouds and it heated the wooden floor of her small eating nook. In the center of the table an African violet drooped pathetically. She touched the dry soil and chastised herself for letting it go without water this long.

This was Saturday, and there was no rehearsal this

afternoon at the hall. The union contract was very explicit about how many free days a week the musicians must receive. Today was the day when Elena could catch up on things around the house. She would water her plants, gather her laundry to send to the cleaners, make an attempt at housecleaning, and work on a composition she had started writing a few weeks ago.

After finishing her soup, Elena washed the bowl, spoon, and saucepan and laid them on the counter to drain. She climbed the stairs to gather her week's worth of laundry and then called the cleaners to come pick it up.

Her house was equipped with a washer and dryer, but she never used them. When her mother was living with her, she had always taken care of those things. Elena had never taken the time to learn the basics of running a house. All of her time was consumed by the piano. It was like a demanding marriage, a husband who insisted upon all of her time and devotion.

In a way it had been good. It had given a center to her life that no earthly relationship could ever have provided. And yet, it had left her peculiarly unbalanced and ill-suited to face the down-to-earth skills of daily living. She was very much like an overly dependent widow who, lost and overwhelmed when tax time rolled around, had no idea which forms to complete.

As she climbed the stairs to the loft, intent on changing the bed linens, the phone rang. She backtracked to the kitchen to pick up the receiver and was surprised to hear her mother's voice. She normally called on Sunday night when the long distance rates were cheaper.

"I was worried about you," Mrs. Shubert offered as answer to Elena's question.

"Why on earth were you worried?"

"Well, I just received your letter today and it didn't sound like you."

Elena had written the letter to her mother three days ago and she had tried to sound casual when she mentioned David Atwell. Obviously her mother had read between the lines.

"So...that young man you knew in college is living there." Mrs. Shubert threw the comment through the wire and followed it with a casual yawn.

Elena wasn't fooled. Her mother wanted the scoop. "Yes. He's a retired football player," she added, maintaining her own cautious reticence.

"I remember him. He was rather special to you at one time, wasn't he?"

"We dated some."

"Ah...well...are you dating him again?"

Elena sighed. "No, Mother. I shouldn't even have mentioned his name. I've only seen him twice."

"Elena," her mother began and Elena held her breath, knowing by the tone of her voice that something significant was forthcoming. "I don't want to meddle, dear. You know I've always tried to stay out of your personal affairs. Lord knows you've always had a mind of your own. But...well, I think a man would add so much meaning to your life and...I just hope you won't discourage Mr. Atwell the way you have other men. There, I've said my piece and that's all I'm going to say about it. Now, how is the weather up there?''

Elena tried not to think about her mother's advice as she picked up the laundry and bundled, tied, and set it by the front door. She didn't want to weigh the merit of her words. She simply didn't want to face that right now. Instead, she sat down on the piano bench and picked up her composition.

The piece she was writing had begun to evolve and grow since she first began working on it a few weeks ago. It had started out purely classical in expression, but had changed almost on its own to a more contemporary sound. It was melancholy at moments, nostalgic, and tranquil. It was the type of music that was best to listen to while sitting before a blazing fire and sipping leisurely on a brandy.

It was during the slower movement, when the music flowed like passion on gossamer wings, that Elena began thinking about David. She wasn't sure if it was the music that made him enter her thoughts or his absence. It was as though this part of the piece had been written with him in mind. As she played it she could feel herself in his arms, taste the sweetness of his lips on hers, know the strength of his flesh and bones.

Her fingers suddenly lifted from the keyboard and began to shake violently. The need for him was screaming through her nerves, crying out for his touch. Why couldn't she forget him for even one hour? She didn't want to feel this need for him. She didn't want to feel this need for anyone. She tried to focus on the piece in front of her, but her mind refused to obey.

It was as if her mind and her body were at war. One would inevitably win, she knew that. But which? As soon as this disturbing thought entered her head, another much more frightening than the first took its place. It sneaked in without her awareness, but it was there all the same. She thought about calling David. What a stupid idea, she told herself. But maybe, just maybe, she should do it. Perhaps if she asked him to make love to her, she could then drive away those forces that seemed bent on controlling her. *Make that thought go away, Elena! Forget it!*

She lowered her hands to her lap, and her head dropped down to her chest. Tears were building under the lids, blurring her vision until she could do nothing but let them fall.

Her life had always had such clear direction. But now she felt as lost as a newborn babe in the woods.

She had her career and yet she didn't have it. She was neither lost nor found. She needed things in her life that she could not even define. Her center seemed to be slipping away as if it were an imploding black hole, sucking everything familiar with its gravitational pull, imprisoning her in an entirely new and unfamiliar dimension.

She pushed herself wearily from the piano bench and walked to the kitchen for another cup of tea. She had been so proud of herself for avoiding David all week and now...now her mind refused to free her from the overwhelming need to see him.

It was Saturday. Maybe she could call him at his hotel, she thought. Then she remembered that today he said there was one of those rare Saturday N.F.L.

games. He was going to be in Pittsburgh announcing it.

After filling her cup with tea, she opened the living room cabinet that housed her tiny portable television, dusted the screen with the hem of her shirt and set it up on the table. As she reached out to turn it on, she paused. She could always insist that his appeal was merely a physical yearning that would go away. But if, on the other hand, she became too involved in his life and in what he was doing, she could not so easily deny his hold over her. Did she want him in her life or did she merely want the physical satisfaction that he could give her?

Closing her eyes beiefly, she cursed herself as a fool then switched on the television.

She had no idea what game he was announcing other than it being a home game for some team from Pittsburgh. She didn't even know what stations she was supposed to receive on the television. The only one she ever watched was the public broadcasting station and she knew the game wouldn't be on that one.

She turned the dial until she saw a football game, listened for several minutes, but didn't recognize David's voice. She turned again, bypassing bowling and figure skating until she found another football game.

It was halftime, so she waited impatiently through the N.F.L. Scoreboard show and through several minutes of commercials until the play resumed.

"If you've just joined us, it's been Pittsburgh all the way. The Steelers, behind the running of Franco Harris who had eighty-five yards so far, have racked up twenty-one points in the first half, while holding

Cleveland to only four first downs.'' A sharp shaft of steel struck the pit of Elena's stomach when she first heard Dave's voice.

"Pittsburgh will be kicking off to Cleveland to start the second half, and the Browns have got their work cut out for them if they want to get back in this ball game.''

There was no mistaking the resonant timbre, the articulate delivery of words. He had a flair for this type of thing; that much was evident.

Though Elena couldn't follow the play, she was enjoying listening to David's voice as he kept up with every move the players made.

"Cleveland's ball, first down on their own thirty-five yard line. Sipe takes the snap and drops back in the pocket. They've got a man open. Beautiful pass! He's got one man to beat. Touchdown Cleveland!''

The richness of his tone as he announced each move the players made soon lulled Elena into a trancelike state. She was looking at the television screen, but she was seeing a playing field twelve years ago. It was cold, but sunny, and she was sitting on the side of the stadium that received the benefit of the sun's rays. Still, she huddled beneath her blanket and curled her toes to stimulate the circulation of blood.

It was her first game and she had only come because David seemed so eager for her to watch him play. The point of the game was clear—the idea was to get the football down to one of those big H's at either end. But the rules and the finer points of play totally eluded her grasp. She cringed every time ten players piled on top of David, and she clapped enthusiastically every time he had the ball and the people around her applauded.

All she could remember was how she had wanted to soothe his every ache, warm his chilled hands with her own, and share in the thrill of his victory.

In her young, eager state of blossoming womanhood Elena knew that she had loved him that day. She had loved him and she had known with a wisdom that surpassed her years that she would have to leave him. She couldn't have two dreams. She couldn't expect life to grant more than one wish and she would have to choose which one she wanted.

She had made the choice, and it had been her music. It alone would carry her through the future. Now here she was twelve years later faced with the same choice. Her life had come full circle...or perhaps a part of her had never really moved beyond that spot in time.

Before, the choice had seemed so obvious. She had been so sure of herself. Now she wasn't sure of anything.

She flipped off the game in agitation. She had to get out of here. Away from those things that tugged her in all directions. The sound of David's voice, the piano, the loneliness.

She grabbed her quilt jacket from the coat closet and pulled on a knitted hat and gloves. She would go to Alexi's house. As much as she detested his supercilious attitude toward her, he might be able to help her. She needed direction, she needed guidance. She could call one of her friends in the orchestra or she could phone Marilee. But Alexi would be even better. As arrogant as he was, he still had the ability to look at things objectively, logically, sifting through the chaff until he found the one grain of truth. Besides, she had to know what he thought about Tina Volkowski's chances with the orchestra.

She walked to the bus stop and waited for the number thirteen bus. She knew from past experience that it would take her to within one block of Alexi's apartment.

As she walked that last block to his apartment, she managed to optimistically toss her problems to the wind. With Alexi's encouragement she knew she could get back on the right track. She could have the sexual relationship her body seemed to crave so with David and she could then concentrate on the next symphony performance, making Alexi, the executive director, and the board members more proud of her than they ever had been. She could even hear the applause in her mind as she imagined bowing humbly before the audience's standing ovation.

Please be home, Alexi, she prayed as she climed the stoop to his front door. *Please,* she begged, needing a solid, stalwart support in her life. Through the closed door she could hear bizarre mideastern music blaring from his stereo. It took several rings before the door finally opened and he peeked his head out.

"Elena, my sweet," he effused, and Elena could tell by the dilation of his pupils and the smell of his breath that he had been smoking something stronger than store-bought cigarettes. "What a coincidence that you should show up at this time." He smiled mockingly. "Do come in, *ma chèrie*."

Elena hated it when he used that French affectation with her. He was of Eastern European descent and his parents had moved the family to France during the war. Shortly afterward they had immigrated to the United States, but Alexi obviously felt that a few French words dropped here and there gave him a sophisticated continental flavor.

Alexi swung open the door wider, revealing the fact that he was wearing only a thin satin robe. As she entered, the stench of marijuana was overwhelming and she could hardly hear herself think because of the grating sitar sound emitting from the speakers.

"Could you turn down the stereo, Alexi? I need to talk to you." Elena was holding her ears as she shouted above the noise.

Alexi snapped his fingers at some unseen person and Elena turned toward whomever he was signaling. Tina Volkowski rose from her overstuffed chair and padded in her short robe and bare feet over to the stereo and turned down the volume, then drifted back to her chair, a smug smile tugging at her lips.

Alexi smiled wickedly at Elena's crestfallen expression. "Something the matter, my little peach?" he cooed insensitively.

Elena stared blankly at Alexi for several long seconds while she tried to still the frantic palpitations of her heart. Tina Volkowski here at Alexi's! Why? *Oh, God. Eléna, don't be stupid. You know why.* Tina was buying her way into the symphony, using her most marketable asset.

She swallowed convulsively, trying to force the sobs down her throat. She glared at Alexi, then turned her eyes in stupefied disbelief upon Tina. She couldn't even make a sound. She knew that if she spoke now her voice would sound hysterical. She had to get out of here! She had to wake up from this nightmare!

God, Alexi! How could you! Elena tore from the room, threw open the front door, and ran down the steps with Alexi's careless laughter following her every step of the way.

She ran to the bus stop but was too agitated to wait for the correct bus to come along. Disregarding the tears that were streaming down her face, she stepped off the curb and hailed the first taxi that drove by. Her hands were shaking so badly she could hardly open the door of the car. This couldn't be happening! This couldn't be real!

Face it, Elena. Don't you realize what has happened? You are out in the cold! It's over. Tina has won. She and her pert little body have sealed your fate.

No! She refused to believe it. There was a logical explanation for Tina being there, she lied to herself. It had nothing to do with the orchestra. . . .

The cabdriver tried to keep his eyes on the road, but the agitated young woman in the backseat kept drawing his attention to the rearview mirror. She was crying and talking to herself as if she had lost her mind. And her hands! Those slim, shaking fingers were moving a mile a minute across her purse as if she were— By God, she looked as if she was playing a piano!

Dave leaned back in his seat on the train as the night sped past his window in a hazy blur. He had planned to wait until Sunday morning to take the train back, but at the last minute he had decided to return tonight. Why, in God's name, was he in such a hurry to return to that cold, unwelcoming city? Elena had made it pretty clear that she didn't want to see him. So why didn't he take the hint and leave her alone?

He smiled and closed his eyes. He knew why. He remembered her eyes and the passion they had held the other day in her kitchen, the fire that was in her when she touched him. That was why.

He breathed deeply to control his pulse rate as his mind centered upon another time with her, when the fire within them had nearly consumed them both.

They had been stretched across the backseat of his Buick, and he remembered noticing that every window in the car was completely fogged from the steam rising from their bodies. In his mind he could still feel the smoothness of Elena's skin as he stroked her back, the way she had trustingly let him remove her sweater and bra.

She smelled so good, so sweet, like honeysuckle on a soft summer evening. He could even remember the taste of her skin, the way his tongue felt on her breasts, the way he ached every time she moved her body under him, like a thousand needles were surging through his bloodstream.

He had wanted to climb inside her, to bring her all around him, make her a part of him. And he had known, when his hand moved between her thighs, how badly she had wanted him.

Dave glanced out the train window, wiping the sweat from his palms onto his jeans. She had no idea what she had done to him every time she touched him, looked at him.

Dave's football coach had known. For him, it was reflected in the poorly executed plays whenever Dave had the ball. It was evident in his lack of concentration during practice sessions. The coach knew and had finally laid down his ultimatum.

It was funny how every time he thought of Elena, even after all the years and all the women, he broke out in the same sweat and pulsated with the equally intense and fervent ache in his loins that he had felt at twenty.

And there was something about her that made him know, beyond a shadow of a doubt, that the need he felt for her went far beyond the physical.

He turned his attention back to the darkening blur of scenery and laughed to himself. No, he didn't have to ask himself why he was going back tonight instead of tomorrow.

Chapter Five

From his place on the stoop outside, the doorbell sounded like a songbird chirping gaily in the new morning light. From her bed inside the house, that same doorbell sounded more like a clanging alarm, a shrieking cry that fit perfectly into the tangled web of her dreams.

Elena stumbled sleepily from the bed, wrapping a thick, quilted robe around her as she walked cautiously down the stairs from her loft. Looking through the beveled glass of the door, she could see David shivering out on the stoop. His hands were thrust deep in his coat pockets, his head lowered against the early morning chill, and he shifted his weight repeatedly from one foot to another.

Oh, damn, she sighed. What on earth was she going to do? Her mind and her body had been at war throughout the night, and still the outcome was unsettled. One part of her wanted to leave him out there on the steps, the door unanswered. That way she could go on with her life the way she had planned it. But another part of her desperately wanted his body in her arms to take away the pain of what she had seen yesterday at Alexi's house. She needed to put into perspective at least one thing in her life. She needed that one touch of reality.

She opened the door slowly and he smiled. That

one endearing smile bolstered her courage more than
anything he could have said. Perhaps her mother was
right. Maybe this was what she needed.

As soon as she opened the door, Dave was struck
by how awful Elena looked. Her eyes were red and
puffy as if from crying. Her skin was sallow and
washed out, and dark blue crescents drooped beneath
her eyes.

There was something else different about her. He
couldn't quite pinpoint it, but it had to do with the
way she greeted him. He had expected her to immediately give some excuse as to why he couldn't
come in. She had to practice, she had to go to the
music hall, anything to keep him away. Instead she
opened the door as if she had been expecting him,
waiting for him.

"You look terrible," he said when she closed the
door behind him.

"You always were an honest soul." She smiled
sadly, and he noticed a difference in her tone of
voice. There was a fatalistic note somewhere adrift in
her statement, as if she were mouthing words that
were written long ago.

She turned away from him, giving herself one last
chance to back out of this plan before she made a
complete and utter fool of herself. Deciding to let her
body win for once in her life, she breathed deeply and
looped her fingers into the sash at her waist.

"I listened to you on the television yesterday," she
whispered softly. When she turned back toward him,
she had untied the sash of her robe. She couldn't help
but notice his surprise, though she wasn't sure if it
was due to her action or her statement.

Dave's eyes jumped from her face to her open robe and back to her face. He wanted to ask her why she had watched the game and what she had thought about his announcing and a million other questions, but his voice suddenly was constricted in his throat. His gaze lowered to the top button of her nightgown. He could feel the heat rising at the back of his neck and his heart began a rhythmic tattoo against his rib cage.

"Will you come upstairs with me, David?" Elena's face looked up at him like a fragile flower reaching for sunlight.

His heart began to thud loudly. God, how he had dreamed of this moment. But something was wrong. Something was missing. What was it? Why couldn't he think straight, for God's sake?

Elena took his hand and began leading him toward the stairway to the loft. She was on the first step, climbing to the second, when he stopped her.

With his hands on her waist he spun her around so their eyes met evenly. "Why, Elena? Why now?" He hated himself for asking the question. He should be following her up the stairs and holding her warm flesh in his arms, not asking stupid questions. But he had to know. He always had to have answers.

She clasped her fingers around his neck and leaned toward him, her lips brushing lightly across the surface of his, spreading featherlight kisses across his cheek and brow. Her hands pressed against his cheeks as she moved back to his mouth, letting her tongue circle his lips the way he had done to her the other day.

Dave's hands tightened on her waist, his fingers

digging into her side as his lips responded to her sensual invitation. Whatever question he had asked her was lost in the air along with all his other thoughts. For now he was only one solid mass of raw nerve endings that cried for satisfaction.

Just as he was about to scoop her up in his arms, he felt her shaking convulsively against him and hot tears spilled from her eyes onto his cheek.

He tried to pull back to see what was the matter, but she was clinging to his neck as she sobbed hysterically and he could do nothing but hold her against him until her weeping subsided.

"Shhh, it's all right, honey. Don't. Don't cry. Shhh."

Elena's fingers dug into his back, holding fast to his strength and quiet affection.

When, after several torturous minutes, she had finally shed all of her tears, she raised her head and wiped the back of her hand across her cheeks. She pulled away from David in embarrassment and walked toward the couch, awkwardly holding her robe closed at her breasts. She curled her legs beneath her in the wicker chair and David followed, sitting close beside her on the couch.

He was leaning forward, his hands clasped between his knees and he watched her intently, waiting for her to explain what in the hell was happening between them.

Sniffling, Elena pulled a tissue from the pocket of her robe and dabbed at her nose, then dropped her hands to her lap where she began twisting the tissue nervously.

"David, I'm sorry. God," she laughed bitterly, "it seems like I'm always apologizing to you."

Dave continued to watch her, afraid to say anything. He wasn't sure he wanted to hear what she had to say. He wasn't sure he wanted to know what kind of game she was playing.

When she was silent for too long, he finally spoke. "Did you not have any intention of following through with your...invitation?" he asked, mentally puzzled and physically frustrated by the twisted turn of events this morning.

"Yes, I did!" she cried. "Whatever else I may be, David, I'm not a tease," she insisted.

"Then what? I don't understand."

She looked at him guiltily, glanced out the windows at the early morning fog, then back at him again.

"I wanted to make love to you, David. I really did. But I thought that once I did, maybe I wouldn't need you so much anymore. I thought...I thought it was just a physical yen I had for you."

Dave quickly stood, shoving his hands into the back pockets of his jeans, and walked to the window. His back was to the room, and Elena had an almost irresistible urge to go to him, to run her palms across the muscular surface between his shoulders, to let them glide down his spine and wrap around his waist.

She looked back down at her hands clenched tightly in her lap, forcing the wayward thoughts from her mind. When he spoke, her head jerked up sharply to stare incredulously at him.

"What did you say?" she asked, stunned.

"I said you were using me as an implement, isn't that right? A mechanical device." His back was still turned toward her, but she could feel the burning anger in his voice.

"David, I—"

He turned to glare at her. "All the time I've thought about you, wondered what it would be like to make love to you, to hold you through the night." His laugh was harsh and bitter. "And you...you want to use me as a human vibrator to purge you of your physical attraction for me." He continued to impale her for several long seconds with his furious stare.

"Damn!" he muttered under his breath, angry strides carrying him toward the door to leave.

His hand was turning the doorknob, his escape at the tip of his fingers. And yet something too forceful to deny held him back. He turned to glance back at Elena who was still sitting in the wicker chair, her head down and her hair falling forward over her face. He should leave. He should walk out and forget he ever knew her. He didn't always have to ask so many questions. Why in hell did he always have to know?

Puffing out his cheeks, he expelled a tortured sigh, striking the frame of the door with his fist as he spun back around to face her.

"Why, Elena? Can you just tell me that?" He walked back over to her and removed his coat for the first time since he had come inside, flinging it angrily on the wicker couch.

"I'm scared, David," she whispered, and he squatted down in front of her to hear her better.

"What did you say?"

She lifted her face to him. "I don't know what I'm doing anymore. I don't know where I'm going. My mind tells me one thing and—and my body another." She looked away quickly, embarrassed. "I don't know what I'm going to do with my life!" she cried.

"I thought you were going to play the piano," he said, trying to maintain a distance in his tone. Yet, that aloof stance was hopeless. He couldn't remain detached from Elena and her problems, no matter how hard he tried.

"I thought so too," she laughed, but her mouth turned down into that despondent crescent. "I think I'm going to be replaced."

"What does that have to do with me? With what happened this morning?" The tinge of bitterness returned to his voice.

She sighed. "I wish I knew, David. I wish to God I knew." She reached out, placing her hands on his shoulders, and felt him automatically stiffen in alert wariness. But she didn't remove them. She had to tell David why she did it. She had to really talk to him. They had been able to talk to each other at one time. Maybe they still could. For the first time in twelve years she looked him directly in the eyes.

"Do you remember how we used to talk about the future? How we were so secure in the knowledge that whatever we wanted would automatically be there for us?"

"I remember." Dave nodded, thinking back to those times in Missouri when they would sit and dream together about the golden promises the world held for them both. They had been so naive! So blind to what life was all about.

"David, I've never wanted to be anything but a concert pianist. I don't know how to be anything else." She prayed silently that he wouldn't laugh at her. She wanted him to try to understand what her life had been like, how contained it had been.

It all sounded so familiar to Dave. Hadn't he said those same words to himself only five months ago? He had never wanted to be anything but a football player. He didn't know how to be anything else.

"You're being replaced by another pianist, is that it?" he asked, subconsciously forgiving her for any frustration she had caused him.

"I think so. She's the niece of one of the symphony directors. She's—she's gifted."

"Well, so are you, Elena," David insisted.

"She's young," Elena answered, as if that said it all.

"Can't you get a job with another orchestra?"

"No one will pick me up if this organization lets me go here. My manager has already hinted that I'm past the break-off age. It's unfair!" she cried.

"Yes, it is." He placed his palms on her thighs, massaging her skin and muscles as he talked. "Life isn't fair, Elena. But it's our fault for not knowing that. Hell, I don't know, maybe our parents should have prepared us more for what lay ahead. But somehow we should have known."

As she watched him she realized that he really did understand exactly what she was talking about. He hadn't laughed at her. He knew. He felt it too.

"Hell, I thought I'd play football forever," he continued. "I was sure I would be another George Blanda. I'd be known as the old man of the league," he laughed. "Football was my life, Elena. I didn't know how to do anything but run down a gridiron with a damn pigskin in my hands."

Elena smiled and stroked the taut muscles of David's shoulders. "Why did you quit?"

"My body grew old before my mind did, I guess. My leg had been hurt so many times and the doctors convinced me that if I didn't give up the game I might end up completely crippled."

"But at least you had another career to fall into."

"You've got to be kidding!" He frowned at her. "I didn't fall into anything—except a month or two of depression. I had to fight tooth and nail to get this announcer's job. You think you've got the only profession that doesn't have a fallback position, but you couldn't be more wrong. Oh, sure, I could have sold insurance or used cars, or taught Little League." He waved his hand absently to dismiss those ideas entirely.

"When I was playing in the N.F.L., people came to me all the time offering terrific positions with their companies, contracts to sell this or that. I thought that if I ever did decide to quit, I would have it made. But you know, when I retired, not one of those deals was reoffered. I was a has-been. Nobody needed or wanted a washout."

"You could never be a washout, David," Elena challenged indignantly.

He shrugged his shoulders. "I know that now. But for a while there I almost believed that I was."

"So how did you get the job on television?" she asked, fascinated now by this common thread that wove between them, binding them together in friendship. Somewhere deep inside of her she registered the fact that it was more than friendship, but she knew that she would have to sort out all of her feelings later when she was alone.

"When I found out about the position," he explained, "I spent a good portion of my savings flying all over the country, talking to everyone connected with the televising of games. I can talk." He grinned sheepishly. "You know that."

Elena suppressed a laugh but agreed with a nod how truthful his self-analysis was.

"So I talked and I talked and I—"

"Talked?" she quipped.

"Incessantly," he replied. "I was sick of hearing myself, to be truthful. But I at least got my foot in the door. Keep in mind, I'm on trial this season. If I work out, I'll receive a contract for next year. If not..." He shrugged.

"You'll sell used cars." She smiled playfully.

"Could be. I'm practicing up for it just in case." He effected a slick, toothy grin. "Hidy-Hi there, friends and neighbors. This is your ole pal, Dave 'Barnstorming' Atwell down here at Wilkins County Chev-ro-let. Damn, we got some mighty fine bargains!"

The tears that coursed down her cheeks were completely dry now and Elena was laughing with delight. Once again Dave had been able to make her forget her troubles for a few minutes. No one else had ever been able to bring her out of her own small sphere of existence except him.

At the same time she wasn't sure if she was grateful to him for that or perturbed that he could make her lose the focus of her life.

"One thing I've learned out of all of this, Elena,"

he added on a serious note, "is that nothing in life is permanent."

"But I honestly don't know what I would do," she cried. "I have a friend who teaches music to grade-schoolers and I know that I couldn't do that. I don't have the patience it takes. Besides, most of the children she teaches don't want to learn to play anyway. Their mothers have pushed them into it."

"You could play in a cocktail lounge somewhere," David suggested, grinning. "You know, the type of place where drunks would drool down onto the keyboard while you play."

"No, I don't know the type of place," she replied arrogantly, adding, "thank God. Really, David, what's left? Other than selling spinet pianos in a warehouse showroom," she laughed. "I mean, honestly, there's nothing I can do!"

"At least you're laughing about it. That's the first step. Your problem, honey, is that you've been living in another century for too long. You eat, drink, breathe, and make love to that piano. You've got to learn to live."

"But I don't want to do anything but play the piano!" she argued.

"That's because you don't know there's anything else to do. Now—" he stood, pulling her up with him "—the first thing you're going to do is get dressed, while I fix us some breakfast. Then we're going to go out and enjoy the day together."

"But I have to practice," she asserted, suddenly wanting to retain what little independence she seemed to have left.

"This is Sunday, a day of rest, Elena. And I know

that somewhere in there—'' he pointed to her skull ''—is the capacity to enjoy the day.''

"No, David, I have to practice." She planted her fists on her waist and stared at him with mutinous determination.

He narrowed his gaze, deliberating long and hard before making his decision. "One hour, Elena. You can practice for one hour and then I'm taking you out of this..." He swept his arms around him. "This mausoleum."

"Mausoleum!" she cried in indignation. "This is my house."

"Yeah," he mumbled. "Well, to corrupt the old cliché—one man's castle is another man's tomb. Now go get dressed."

She knew she was going to be punished for this dereliction of her duty, this irresponsible shirking of practice. She was supposed to practice. That's what a musician did. Somewhere down the line she would surely be punished. But right now she was more afraid of arguing with David than with what would happen later.

She hurried up the stairs and pulled her plaid wraparound skirt and navy blue sweater from the closet. She laid them across the chair then went into the bathroom to wash her face. While she applied a light touch of makeup, she could hear David slamming cabinet doors downstairs in the kitchen and mumbling grouchily to himself.

"Elena!" She nearly jammed her mascara wand into her eye when she heard him shout at her from the bottom of the stairs. She ran to the balcony and leaned over.

"What?" she asked, wondering why he was looking up at her with such a perturbed expression.

"Where is your food? There is nothing in your refrigerator, nothing in your cabinets, nothing anywhere." He was trying to sound stern but it was so difficult when she insisted on leaning over the railing that way, her hair trailing down over the edge like Rapunsel, her robe flaring open at the neck.

"There's some bread in the refrigerator. I remember seeing it yesterday."

"Bread! That's it, bread?"

"What do you want, David?"

"I said breakfast. That usually means bacon and eggs, toast, maybe some hashbrowns or grits."

"Grits!" she giggled. "Why, I do declare, Rhett Butler, the things you say could turn a lady's head."

"Go ahead and make fun, Yankee," he said, pointing at her with his index finger. "But you haven't lived until you've tried my cheese grits. Now, where's the nearest grocery store?"

Elena straightened up and frowned. "Let's see, there's a little market about a block from here. But that's mostly just fruits and vegetables, a few canned goods."

"Grocery store, Elena. I want a regular grocery store."

"I don't know, David."

"Where do you buy your food?" He was literally amazed that anyone wouldn't know where a grocery store was.

"I usually eat out. I'm not very proficient at domestic things," she apologized.

"Obviously." He sounded disgusted. "Well, finish getting dressed and we'll go find one. If I teach you nothing else, you are going to learn how to eat properly.''

Elena squatted down behind the railing, her hands on the upper banister and her head pressed against the columnar bars. She peered through seductively at David. "If that's all you're going to teach me, Rhett darlin', I may not come downstairs.''

Dave lifted an eyebrow at her. He placed one foot on the bottom stair and followed it with the other, slowly mounting the stairs by inches, forcing Elena to run frantically into the bathroom, locking the door behind her. When she was safely locked in, she crossed her arms in front of her, hugging herself and giggling like an adolescent on her first date.

"I'll drive, if you don't mind.'' He smiled impishly, patting his chest. "My heart can only take so much trauma in one day.''

"Suit yourself,'' she replied haughtily. "Heaven forbid I should be accused of frightening the old and feeble.''

"Cute, Elena. Now, let's see, where shall we begin?''

They drove for twenty minutes before they found a grocery store that was open. Dave glanced at Elena as he parked the car and noted the wide-eyed expression on her face as if she were embarking on some new and wondrous adventure.

"This is a grocery store.'' Dave pointed like a tour guide.

"Really,'' she drawled, pretending to be bored out of her mind. "How bourgeois.''

"Come on." He held the door for her. "It's time you joined the masses in their daily toil."

"Now, this is a pound of bacon." Dave held the package up before her when they stopped in front of the meat counter. "It comes from a hog."

Elena patted Dave's flat, taut stomach, and murmured caustically, "And when it's cooked, it goes right back into a hog. Now, if you don't cut out the homemaking lesson, we are not going to have time for anything else today."

"Look, I figure we'd better start with the basics. How you've managed to survive for five months without your mother is beyond me. How can you gain weight on what little you eat?"

"Every time I breathe, calories surge into my body," Elena complained as she watched the shopping cart fill with food. "If I eat all of this, I won't fit on the piano bench, and the audience won't be able to distinguish me from the instrument I'm playing."

"The idea," Dave explained patiently, "is to eat the right things. You need protein, vitamins. Look." He held up a package of sardines. "Vitamin E."

"What does vitamin E do for you?" she asked innocently.

He narrowed his gaze on her, remembering how she tried to seduce him this morning. "Forget it, you don't need it." He threw the package back on the shelf.

Don't we have enough? she wondered, tiring of this escapade already. If grocery shopping was what the real world was like, she didn't want any part of it.

Dave continued his lecture on nutrition as they

drove home and fixed a huge breakfast in her kitchen. Elena tried to hide her boredom with the whole ordeal.

She didn't want to learn to cook. She didn't want to learn to shop. She was a pianist and, regardless of how impermanent David believed things to be, she was not yet ready to give up her career in defeat. As long as there was a chance that she could hold out against the Tina Volkowskis of this world, she would do it.

Dave held out a plate heaped with food toward Elena. "This is breakfast," he said.

Groaning inwardly, Elena took the plate from his hands.

After breakfast Dave held to his bargain to let her practice for one hour. He tried to mold his body into a suitable position on the wicker couch and wondered how anyone could get comfortable on one of those things. He looked at Elena's small body perched so ladylike on the piano bench and an image of her lying beneath him on the couch, her legs wrapped around his thighs, stirred crazily in the sexual core of his body. He knew he had better stop thinking of her that way or he would never be able to let her practice the piano.

He clasped his hands behind his head and stretched out halfway across the floor with his feet crossed at the ankles, trying to force a casualness in his observation of her at the piano. But every time her white thigh was exposed when she lifted a foot to press the pedal, warm sensations rushed through him and he felt an uncontrollable tightening in the lower half of his body.

His eyes were fixed on her in a state of pleasure-pain. So many little things about her excited him. The back of her neck underneath that mass of chestnut hair, the vulnerability of her hand fluttering uselessly in the kitchen a few minutes ago.

She was so much softer and more pliable than other women he had known, and in his daydream fantasy her white flesh begged to be molded by his hands.

Elena could feel the prickly heat along her left side where David's eyes struck her. She tried to disassociate herself from him as she did with an audience.

She had learned at an early age that you must not think of the audience out there watching and listening to you. There were always going to be distractions in the audience, children fidgeting, men coughing. But a good pianist must become so lost in her music that she played only for herself, the toughest critic of all.

That part had rarely bothered her. She had always been able to isolate herself on stage without feeling overly nervous. So why was she now having such trouble removing David from her mind? She had to fight to keep her eyes on the sheet music and away from his face. And she couldn't help but worry over what he would think of her and her playing.

Pulling in a deep, even breath to slow the racing of her pulse, Elena began practicing the *Peer Gynt Suite* for the program she and the orchestra would be performing at the university next week. It was a performance in the young people's concert series and was also a benefit concert from which all proceeds would join a fund for the relief of world hunger.

As she played she was soon lost in the lilting fantasy of the piece before her. She knew the entire suite by heart, but she kept the music before her in practice sessions to ensure the proper tonality and tempo.

The first suite began with the pastoral "Morning Mood." The sweetness of the music, though written for an Egyptian theatrical scene, always suggested to Elena a tranquil, sunlit morning in the towering, heaven-kissed regions of Norway. And that is the way she fingered it—as if she were standing at the bank of a teal-blue fjord, gazing upward into the surrounding velvet green mountains capped with a light film of snow.

David closed his eyes as he listened to the music. He remembered this suite so well. Elena had played it for a recital he had attended in college, and because of that, it had always been one of his favorites.

It told the story of Henrik Ibsen's *Peer Gynt*, a self-seeking rogue who fritters away his days in dreams, shunning work at all costs. He weaves tall tales with himself as the conquering hero, making him the laughingstock of his neighbors and the despair of his widowed mother, Ase.

Crashing a wedding party of two of the villagers, Peer tries to attract attention to himself with one of his farfetched tales. Only one woman, the lovely Solveig, is interested. But Peer is attracted to her for only a moment. Instead, he abducts the bride, Ingrid, and carries her off into the mountains, where he later abandons her.

Now a notorious outlaw, Peer roams about the Norwegian mountains with wild shepherd girls and diabolical trolls. He stumbles into the kingdom of the

Mountain King where he becomes involved with the Woman in Green, daughter of the Mountain King. When the situation becomes too intense, he escapes the kingdom and builds a hut for himself high up in the mountains.

Solveig, in the meantime, has given up her home and her family to share Peer's lonely life. He is greatly touched by her devotion, but soon the restless cravings stir within him and he again leaves.

He makes and loses fortunes in America and later meets Anitra, a beautiful Bedouin girl in Egypt.

Finally he is a tired and disillusioned old man when he returns home through storm and shipwreck. The only one who is there to welcome him is Solveig, who still believes in him and has vowed to love him unto death.

Dave opened his eyes and watched Elena. She was now playing "Solveig's Song," in which the woman pours out her heart in belief that Peer will return someday. Elena's fingers flowed in tranquil andante, moving faster in allegretto before slowing down once again for the final passage.

The story was like them in a way, Dave reflected. They both had a lot of Peer Gynt in them and perhaps a little of Solveig. They had both been self-seeking, denying the need for a stable, faithful relationship. They had both had the restless stirrings to seek out those things they could never have. Now Dave was ready to come home.

But one question remained. Was Elena ready to come home?

Chapter Six

Dave stood up, stretching and walking leisurely about the room while Elena penciled notations onto the sheet music in front of her.

He walked up behind her, laying his hands on her shoulders and bending to kiss the top of her head. He didn't see the smile that softened her features, but he felt the loosening of her muscles under his fingers as the tension eased from her body.

"What's that?" He picked up a stack of music staff paper that was punctuated by hand-drawn notes, time signatures, and tempo marks. Other elements of notation were scrawled haphazardly in upper and lower margins.

"Oh, it's nothing." She quickly covered the stack with a Schirmer book of finger exercises.

"Are you composing?" Dave asked with surprise, as he casually picked up the Schirmer and tossed it aside. "Are you?"

"It's just something I dabble in," she explained with embarrassment. "It's really—"

"Will you play it for me?" He picked up the stack, handed it to her, and sat down on the bench beside her. There was no request in his voice or in his actions. He was expecting her to play.

For one defiant moment she looked at him as if to refuse his request, then softened when she noticed the enthusiasm that was behind his eyes. She had never played her own music for anyone. She had never taken it seriously, nor had she thought that it was good enough to play for anyone else. David wasn't a musician, but still, he had always loved good music and she supposed she did need a critic.

"Will you be honest?" she asked, praying silently that he wouldn't be too honest.

Dave effected his most stern expression. "The work will be valued on its redeeming social value," he replied loftily.

"Then I'm in big trouble." Elena turned with resignation to the composition she had lined up on the piano. Lifting her fingers to the keyboard, she sighed and began.

From the moment her fingers struck the first key, Dave could feel the excitement emanating from her body. Each chord, each rapid scale run, each note, was wrought from something inside of her. He had listened to her play the classics and he knew how talented she was. But this was different. There was something so moving and personal in the contemporary sounds she was creating under her fingertips, as if she were putting her own life story into music.

She stopped in the middle, playing back over the last couple of measures. Grabbing her pencil, she made a revision, tried it out, and resumed playing.

"Sounds great, Elena," Dave said as she continued on.

"I've got an idea for some lyrics to go with it," she inserted, still sounding embarrassed over what she had created.

When she finished playing, she quickly stacked the

papers and dropped them in a pile beside the piano. "Anyway—" she shrugged uncomfortably "—that's it."

Dave grabbed her arm, halting her nervous shuffling of the music. "Elena, that is terrific! You are incredible!"

Elena looked away, embarrassed.

"I mean it. You could be another Burt Bacharach."

"It's just something I do for fun, David. I don't plan on doing anything with it."

"Why not?" He was not only surprised, he was aghast. "You can't let that talent go to waste!"

"David, I'm a pianist. I'm not a composer or a songwriter. It's a hobby. I told you that."

"What are you going to do if the orchestra lets you go? You're going to have to find some avenue for your talents."

Elena spun around furiously, glaring at him for reminding her of her tenuous relationship with the symphony. "I'm not ready to give up yet, David. They haven't said they're letting me go," she added icily.

Dave shook his head as he watched her go to the kitchen for a refill of tea. She just couldn't admit that the end was inevitable. She still clung to some irrational thread of hope, that naive belief that her life was not meant to be altered.

There was certainly nothing wrong with hope or with a positive outlook, he reminded himself. The only problem was that when she lost the game, which eventually she would, the defeat she would suffer was going to be a terrible thing for her to accept.

What would happen to her then?

That afternoon Elena went on the first picnic she had been on since college. At David's insistence they bought a large picnic basket, packed it with wine and cheese, a loaf of French bread, and some sliced ham.

It was cold in the park, but jeans, heavy jackets, and a wool blanket to sit on provided adequate cover for warmth.

"Lie back and look up through the bare branches of the trees," David directed her. "Now, tell me, Elena Shubert, how does it feel to do absolutely nothing at all?"

She wasn't sure how it felt. She was aware of a sense of guilt, to be sure. She knew she should be home practicing the Dvořák *New World Symphony* for next week's performance. There were still several passages in the piece that needed work.

But beyond the pangs of guilt she wasn't sure what she was feeling. She was so used to filling up her hours with music projects that she never took the time to experience all the things that most people enjoyed.

"You haven't lived," David had said earlier. Perhaps he was right. Still lying back on the blanket, she reached for his hand. It seemed so right being here with him. His pale green eyes sparkled under the circular patch of sunlight. The strong column of his neck appeared even more sturdy above the collar of his tan jacket, and the broad spread of chest tempted her hands once again. His hand in hers was rough but gentle and she longed to feel its touch upon her bare flesh.

The afternoon idly drifted by with the nomadic clouds above. Dave and Elena talked about the things they had done in the years they had been apart.

Dave told her about some of the people he had met and the cities in which he had played. He entertained her with eccentric character traits of some of his teammates and shocked her with admissions of the dirty tricks the teams occasionally resorted to, such as smearing the offensive linemen's jerseys with motor oil so that they were less easily thrown aside by the defense.

Elena told David about some of the performances that had been held in outlying areas and small towns where speaker systems squealed throughout the entire performance. She told him about the time she had a thirty second memory lapse in the middle of a Brahms concerto while performing before an audience of musicians.

It was as though they were both trying to catch up on all the lost years when they went their separate ways, and as if they were trying to pretend that they had never been apart.

By evening they had exhausted their vocal cords, their memories, and—because they had been eating all afternoon—their appetites.

When they were driving home, Dave slowed in front of one of the more luxurious hotels in the city and asked, "Do you mind if we stop at my hotel for a few minutes? I'm expecting a call from New York, and if it has already come in, I need to call back before too late."

"Sure." She smiled, feeling warm and agreeable after so much wine. She leaned back against the upholstery and closed her eyes, letting the monotonous hum of the motor and warm breath of the heater lull her into a semihypnotic state.

When Dave pulled into the underground parking lot of the hotel, Elena opened her eyes. He eased the car into a parking space, switched off the motor, and leaned against the steering wheel to watch Elena, his mouth curving upward in a soft smile.

"You look tired," he crooned, gently brushing her face with the back of his hand.

"All this leisure time has worn me out." She stretched and yawned.

Dave slapped the steering wheel and opened his door. "I know just what will wake you up," he declared as he helped her out of her side of the car. "Come on."

With a purposeful stride that she had trouble matching, Dave led Elena up the stairs from the parking lot, through the hotel lobby, where he checked at the desk for any messages, and into the swirling phantasmagoria of the hotel's disco.

"I'm not dressed for this," Elena argued, ransacking her brain for excuses.

"Nonsense," Dave stated, never slowing his stride for a moment.

"I can't dance, David!" Elena pulled back on his hand, trying to halt his onward plunge through the crowd.

"Sure you can," he dismissed her second argument without even glancing at her. "Anyone can do this kind of dancing."

The blaring music was deafening, the low, rhythmic beat of drums vibrating upward through the floor. Above their heads, a glass ball rotated slowly, casting abstract patterns of light over the gyrating couples.

Dave pulled her onto the dance floor, making a small space for them. As he began dancing with a proficiency and grace that contradicted his size, Elena made an effort to do the same. But after a moment she gave up, feeling stupid and clumsy.

"I can't do this, David. I feel like an idiot!"

"You look like everybody else out here," he laughed. "Look around you, Elena. Do you see anyone who looks even remotely normal?"

She smiled sheepishly and tried again. Wrapping his arms around her waist, Dave pulled her next to him, guiding her to the rhythm of his body.

She felt a primitive, unifying heat rising between their bodies, warming her skin and shading her cheeks a dark rose. The wine, the music, the beat, the lights, and the rhythmic undulating of her body with Dave's cast a sensuous spell over her.

Her hands traveled up his arms and looped around his strong neck and she felt his mouth brushing against her throat as she tilted her head back, pressing the lower half of her body closer to his.

"Come with me to my room, Elena," Dave breathed urgently into the hair behind her ear.

He cupped her face in his hands, his eyes flaming with the persuasive question, and Elena felt no resistance within her to deny him or herself this pleasure any longer. He smiled, adding, "I've got a tape recorder and we can play some Debussy or Chopin. A little night music," he whispered huskily.

Her body was filled with electrical impulses, arcing wildly in the lower part of her body, and she regretted having to part for even as long as it took to go to his room.

But Dave wasn't as worried about their temporary parting as he was about getting her to his room in the shortest possible time. He grabbed her hand and pulled her off the dance floor, again making her keep up with his longer and faster strides.

As they left the grinding sounds of the disco behind them, Elena was struck by the peaceful silence and tranquil beauty of the lobby. She hadn't been as aware of it when they had first come into the hotel. But now her senses were vibrating with life and she was acutely aware of every little detail.

Glass elevators dominated the lobby, but surrounding them were soft-cushioned seating arrangements and lots of tall potted plants. As they crossed the marble floor toward the elevators, indistinct sounds from various conversations drifted toward them.

Elena leaned into Dave's body, and he wrapped his arm protectively around her. She felt so good, so incredibly alive for the first time in such a long time. She smiled at him as he punched the button for the elevator.

Glancing thoughtfully about the room, she felt a frigid shaft of ice splinter the warm sensual nimbus that had been floating about her head. She was no longer thinking about David's arms around her, about the heat that had radiated between them only moments before. Instead, she was staring at the group of people who walked into the hotel from the street. One of the directors from the symphony was holding the door open for the members of the board, including Tina's aunt, Eunice Buchanan. The women were dressed in their stylish minks and low-heeled pumps, the men in three-piece suits and wing tips.

Elena felt another icy tremor pass through her and a raw distrust clutched her nerves as she stared at the man who was with them. She was sure she knew him from somewhere. But her mind, so acutely aware of every sensation of the universe only a moment ago, could not place the face.

She didn't realize that she had grasped David's arm and was holding him back away from the open elevator while she continued to wrestle with the problem of who this man was and why he was with the directors. The rolling undulations of desire that had filled her mind and body only minutes before were now beached upon the dry shore of reality. The dilemma of her career and her music was all that was allowed a foothold in her conscious thoughts.

Then it came to her. The man was Jerard Williams, the famous conductor with the Waldheim Philharmonic. Yet, knowing who he was did not explain what he was doing with the directors of this symphony. And where, she wondered suspiciously, was Alexi?

As Elena pondered these questions Dave leaned close to whisper a reminder of where they were going. He was puzzled by the change in her eyes, by their sudden metamorphosis from smoldering glow to passionless glaze.

Elena was unaware of his bewilderment. Her mind no longer on David, she was wondering what this conductor was doing here and in what way it might concern her or her position with the orchestra.

"David, come with me a minute." Her voice became a bubble of excitement. "See those people over there?" She pointed to the small cluster heading toward the restaurant.

"Yes?" So what? he thought distastefully. His mind was trained possessively on only two people—David and Elena. He didn't want any more interruptions.

"Those are the directors of the symphony. That man in the blue velvet jacket is Jerard Williams. Let's go meet him." She began pulling him toward the entrance to the restaurant.

"Elena, do you really want to do this now? Couldn't you meet him—whoever he is—some other time?" Dave couldn't hide the tinge of annoyance in his voice.

Her gaze jumped to his face. "Oh, David, I'm sorry. But please. I don't know why but I have this feeling that something...strange is going on with the symphony and I need to find out what it is. Please, it will only take a minute."

She stared up at him with wide, pleading eyes and he felt his resistance wearing away. He was still annoyed, but if it didn't take long and made her feel more relaxed, then he could wait a few more agonizing minutes.

He glanced down past her face at the sweater that curved across her breasts with tantalizing invitation, the thin waist where the rib-knit hem cinched tightly. He wanted to pull her hips back into the saddle of his, the way they had been a few minutes ago on the dance floor. But instead he exhaled slowly and with a ragged sound, nodding his acquiescence to Elena and

letting her lead him across the floor in the opposite
direction of the elevators—and his room.

Catching up with them before they were seated at
their table, Elena greeted the directors she had come
only recently to distrust.

"Elena, my dear," crooned Eunice Buchanan.
"How delightful to see you."

Elena's gaze jumped from Mrs. Buchanan's eyes
to her mouth. She looked sincere, but Elena couldn't
be sure. Before Tina came into the picture, Elena had
always liked Mrs. Buchanan and assumed that the
feeling was reciprocated. But now she just didn't
know. After all, the woman had arranged for the
board to hear Tina play. Elena returned the smile,
hoping that her insecurity did not show.

"This is my friend, David Atwell." She looped her
arm through Dave's as she introduced him to the
four directors. "And you're Mr. Williams, aren't
you?" She extended her hand to the conductor, unaware of the anxious glances that passed among the
board members.

"Yes, I am," Jerard Williams answered compla-
cently in a voice that was stiff with condescension.
But beyond the voice, beyond the arrogant smile,
Elena was aware of a laser heat that emanated from
Jerard Williams's eyes and blazed a searing path
through her skin.

He was not an attractive man, his head too large
for his slim neck and his features too large for his
head. But there was a charismatic appeal about him
that must have accounted for his extraordinary repu-
tation with women. Still, his intense stare left Elena
bewildered and somewhat frightened.

"Mr. Williams is in town on business," Tina's aunt chirped, "and so of course we insisted that he join us for dinner."

It was the narrowed look in Jerard Williams's eyes that told her Mrs. Buchanan was lying. Why, Elena didn't know. But it was obvious that the directors were taking the conductor out to dinner for some reason other than as a social amenity. Again her thoughts drifted to Alexi and his noticeable absence.

"You are the pianist." Jerard interrupted Elena's thoughts in a controlled, emotionless voice. He lifted her hand to kiss it, his mouth leaving as flat an imprint as his voice had, but his eyes remained fixed upon her in ruthless and sagacious regard.

Elena felt Dave's arm tighten around her waist and sensed, in the savage heat that began to rise from his skin, his possessive distrust of Jerard Williams.

"Perhaps Miss Shubert would like to join us?" Jerard totally ignored Dave's presence as he offered the invitation.

Elena didn't fail to notice the stricken expressions tugging worriedly at each director's face. "I'm sure that Elena and her young man have other plans for the evening," Mrs. Buchanan quickly asserted, her voice quavering with anxious vibrato tones. The look she cast at Elena was devoid of information, giving her no clue as to where she fit into this private scheme.

Elena glanced at Jerard Williams and wondered what role he played in all of this. That intense heat was still radiating from his eyes, and she couldn't help but ponder how much influence he could have over her career.

"Ah, well," Jerard spoke in those same even, emotionless tones. "Perhaps later." He smiled crookedly at Elena, leaving no doubt in her mind that his invitation included much more than dinner.

Forcing herself to appear untroubled, she said good night and watched as the group was seated at its table. But her mind was on the famous conductor and the disturbing invitation she had read in his eyes. Still holding on to Dave's arm, she looked up at him and found anything but invitation in his expression.

His mouth and jaw were clenched tightly with barely suppressed frustration and his eyes had turned cold and pale.

He had been aware of the change that had come over Elena since the board members first walked into the hotel. And he had also been very aware of the effect the conductor had upon her.

He searched his own mind for conclusions, wondering if his feelings for Elena had been based on a memory, on something that was no longer there. Maybe her career really was the only thing that was important to her, and perhaps he was nothing more in her life than a brief return to the past.

"It's funny." Dave scowled down at her. "But suddenly music in the night seems like the loneliest sound in the world."

Chapter Seven

As the clock vigilantly ticked off the hours, Elena's metronome, perched insolently on the piano bench, was waiting to tick off the beats of music. She stared guiltily at the piano before turning back to her friend.

"I'm just not ready to roll over and play dead."

"Elena, for God's sake!" Marilee retorted with disgust. "Just because you have a man does not mean you have to give up everything else in your life."

"I don't have a man," Elena argued.

Marilee sighed impatiently. They had been over the same thing for the past half hour. "Okay, Elena, thinking about a man. You can think about a man and think about your music at the same time."

"Maybe you can, but I can't. Don't you understand, I may lose my position with the orchestra!"

"You say that as if it is the end of the world. There are other things, you know."

"Not for me, Marilee."

Marilee finished her last sip of tea and set the cup down with a clatter. "Well, what about David? What about your relationship with him?"

"I don't know that I want a relationship with him." Elena frowned. "I mean I do, but I don't. Does that make sense?"

"No." Marilee's mouth was pursed in annoyance.

"I don't think I can have a good relationship with a man—with David—and maintain my career. Both take too much out of me. Both need to be nurtured, supported, indulged."

She had known this when she was eighteen and had come to terms with it then. She had dealt with it at that time in the only way possible. She had been right! Regardless of what David might think now, neither of them could have maintained a loving relationship with each other at that time.

Twelve years ago they had to go their own ways, had to prove that they could realize their dreams. They would never have been satisfied with each other if they hadn't at least tried to accomplish their life-long ambitions.

"I was meant to do exactly what I'm doing, Marilee. I'm happy with my life."

Marilee gaped at Elena in disbelief. "That has got to be the biggest bunch of bull I have ever heard."

Elena cleared her throat self-consciously and quickly picked up her cup and saucer to carry into the kitchen. She was happy, dammit! Why couldn't Marilee see that? And why couldn't David?

She rinsed the cup and set it upside down on the drainboard. With her hands resting on the counter's edge she stared gloomily out the window overlooking the back garden. If she was honest, she would have to admit that something was missing in her life. No, someone was missing.

It wasn't just a physical relationship that was needed to fill the void. Those types of encounters were never hard to find. It was something more lasting that she wanted, someone to share the little things with.

"Are you going to choose between the two?" Marilee walked into the kitchen carrying her own cup and saucer.

"What do you mean?" Elena frowned as she took the cup and placed it in the sink.

"I mean are you going to choose between your career and David? You said you couldn't have both, so you're obviously going to have to pick one over the other."

"I'm already married to my music, Marilee. I won't be unfaithful to it."

Marilee shook her head slowly, a peeved expression twisting her mouth sideways. "Are you going to tell David?"

Elena pulled in a dry breath and bit her lower lip. She would have to, she supposed. She didn't want to lead him on. The sooner she told him, the better it would be for both of them. She had made her choice at eighteen and it had been the right one then. Surely it was today!

"Yes, I will tell him."

Dave glanced up from the player stats he was studying. He stretched his long legs and propped them on the coffee table in front of the couch. Leaning his head back against the cushions, he closed his eyes and scowled at the indignity of loving someone who didn't love him.

When he first saw Elena after so many years, he wondered exactly what it was that kept drawing him to her even when she insisted that she wasn't interested. He thought perhaps it was a matter of pride. Some unfinished business, like a loose thread that needed to be tied. Loose ends in one's life were terribly messy and needed to be taken care of.

Elena Shubert had been dangling like an unkempt thread since he was twenty, brushing against his subconscious, weaving surreptitiously into his relationships with other women, tickling his fantasies in the middle of the night. Snipping it off would have been the quickest way to set his life in order. However, once he saw her after so many years, he knew he couldn't put an end to it that quickly. Perhaps, he thought in the beginning, if he could simply take her to bed—that would tie off the loose end that had been bothering him for so many years. After all, except for that final physical commitment, they had been as close as two lovers could be.

But again, he hadn't been able to do it that expeditiously. After that morning in her kitchen when she reached up to stroke his cheek, a look of such need in her eyes, he knew it would take more than a brief physical encounter with her to satisfy him.

Dave shifted uncomfortably on the couch. Damn love! Who needed it? He hadn't intended on falling in love, especially with someone who didn't love him. There had been lots of women in his life, ones who came and went without leaving a trace of substance behind them.

There had been the football groupies, those young and not-so-young women who were impressed by the team jersey and not by who was inside it. Then there had been the ones whom his friends had arranged for him to date. Some had even been able to make him forget that irksome loose thread for a little while. It was funny. He had loved them while they made him forget Elena and afterward he had hated them for the very same reason.

But one essential fact did remain: Elena was not interested in any permanent relationship with him. And after what happened at the hotel the other night, he couldn't for the life of him figure out why he should give a damn.

If he thought for a minute that she really didn't care at all about him, he would leave her alone. He would try to forget what could have been between them and learn to get along with what was. But something intangible in the way she looked at him made him believe that she felt more than she would admit even to herself.

She was scared and he knew how that felt. Her whole life was shifting tracks and she wasn't ready to accept it. But if she'd only let him help her. After all, he had been through it. She was a lost little girl, still clutching her dreams around her like a pacifying blanket, afraid to wake up and join the grown-up world of reality. She believed that she could exist as an island unto herself. She didn't know that everyone—even Elena Shubert—needed someone to care for her.

Dave forced himself to pick up the sheets containing the game statistics, knowing he had to get his mind off Elena. If he wanted to hang on to this new job, he had better start doing some of the work involved. He also had to start looking for a permanent place to live. He couldn't keep chasing after Elena. He wouldn't. Some things a person has to find out for herself. If she needed him, she would come to him. He would simply have to wait.

His shoulders sagged with the burden of reality when he thought about how difficult that wait was going to be.

That afternoon, when Elena arrived at the music hall, she was startled and perplexed to find Jerard Williams standing in as conductor for Alexi. The other members of the orchestra were as mystified as she, and when she questioned some of them about it, they merely shrugged their shoulders.

Although most of the musicians were used to Alexi's supercilious air and thunderous diatribes, no one was prepared for the quiet deprecation that emanated from every syllable Jerard Williams uttered.

It was as though each of them should feel humbled that this genius nonpareil would bestow his gift of orchestration upon them. And when he cast his blistering gaze upon Elena, she felt a penetrating chill run from the back of her neck down to her toes.

During the rehearsal session Jerard would intersperse his rather digressive lecture with repetitive taps of his baton on the podium.

"Piano will play the cadenza at the end of the concerto. Elena, remember to use rubato on those prolonging chords, and hold the descending thirds." Elena nodded her head in understanding, although Jerard was perusing his sheet music rather than looking at her.

"Now then, strings," he continued, rapping the podium with his baton as he addressed the string quartet of the orchestra. "Right before this cadenza in the first movement, the composer is calling for leggiero. Elegant, graceful, some vibrato. As for the wind section—''

Elena silently ran her fingers across the keyboard without depressing any notes. She was trying hard to concentrate on what was being said, but all she could think about was why Jerard Williams was here instead of Alexi. Surely Alexi hadn't been replaced. If Jerard was going to take over as conductor on a permanent basis, what effect would this have on her position with the symphony?

''Miss Shubert? Elena!'' Jerard snapped imperiously. ''Are we boring you?''

Elena blushed, stammering, ''No, of course not. I'm sorry.''

Jerard's glare flashed from hot to cold, turning Elena's insides upside down. She tried to make sense of the unspoken signals he was sending her but, like the other night at the hotel, she could not decipher the message.

When he again spoke, the bitter chill had returned to his voice and eyes. ''Would you please pull your head out of the clouds long enough to practice this last movement with us?''

Fearful of subtle undercurrents that were pulling her life into a flow that she could no longer control, Elena lifted her hands to the keyboard and listened passively to the orchestral strains for her cue.

By the time the rehearsal was over, Elena was exhausted. Not only was the practice itself rigorous, but Jerard's exhaustive demands put an added drain on her nerves. She wanted nothing more than to go home, take a long, relaxing bath, and go to bed early.

There was to be a performance tomorrow afternoon at one of the high schools and tomorrow night at the music hall, so she would need all the rest she could get.

As she left the stage she was aware of Jerard Williams watching her, following every step she made with an electrified, raking gaze.

"It was simply bad judgment on my part," Alexi was saying as he packed the belongings from his office into cardboard cartons. "When the little hussy found out I wouldn't endorse her for your position, she ran to her dear auntie crying rape, and the old prig came at me like a raving banshee."

Elena was leaning against the wall, watching him sadly and listening to the reason for his dismissal. Dressed in her long severe black dress, she had just finished the performance at the high school and would be going on stage here at the music hall in fifteen minutes.

She had come to Alexi's office when one of the other musicians mentioned that he was in here packing his belongings. Wild rumors had been buzzing all day about him being fired, and Elena still could not believe it. She had to talk to him and find out for herself if it was really true.

"They're letting you go for that?" she cried, realizing for the first time what a good conductor he was to work for.

Alexi glanced at her with one of his typically scathing looks. "They are not letting me go, my love. They are canning me!"

"What are you going to do, Alexi?"

"You're concerned, Elena darling?" Alexi sarcastically asked. "How touching."

"I am concerned," she answered honestly, feeling sorry for this cynical man and his flippant attempts to cover a basic insecurity.

He looked at her face carefully and narrowed his gaze. Letting down his guard, he smiled and believed her. "Yes, I think you are. Well, not to worry. I've been asked to come to Saint Louis and guest conduct. Perhaps they will pick me up. Who knows?" he added on a note of unconcern.

"What about me, Alexi?" Elena was looking down at her hands, needing but not wanting to know what was going to happen to her position with the symphony. Without Alexi she might not stand a chance of holding out against Tina Volkowski.

"What about you?" he asked uncomprehendingly.

"Am I too going to be canned?"

"How should I know what those lunatics will do?" He shrugged. "You play circles around little Tina. But if her aunt has her way. . . Well, Mrs. Buchanan is the one I would be concerned about if I were you, not Tina."

"But I always thought Mrs. Buchanan liked me."

Alexi frowned at her. "Don't be naive, Elena. What or whom a person likes and what she feels she must do are two entirely different things. Just hang in there and do your best," he advised.

Feeling not the least bit reassured, Elena sighed and walked over to her conductor. "Thank you, Alexi. I've enjoyed working with you." She held out her hand to shake his, but surprising them both, he wrapped her in a fatherly embrace.

"Like hell you have," he laughed, pulling back and holding her at arm's length. "I've been hard on you, Elena, but it's because I knew if I was, then you would perform better. You have a gift, but like scores of other talented people, they have not developed it fully. You will never be a great pianist. You must accept that. But I tried to bring out all that you had to give." He shrugged again and smiled gently at her for the first time. "I think I succeeded at that."

"Good-bye, Alexi." Elena wiped away a single tear from her eye and walked slowly out of the office, heading toward the stage, where she could hear the other members of the orchestra tuning up their instruments, toward the stage that had consumed so many years of her life.

As she walked over to where Jerard Williams was waiting in the wings with Eunice Buchanan and her niece, she heard him mutter, "There she is." Tina's hair was pulled back in one long braid and she wore an empire-styled dress with Peter Pan collar and lace cuffs.

God, Elena thought with disgust. Why didn't she try to look her age?

The two women, one old and powerful, the other young and ambitious, smiled at Elena, and she noticed that only Mrs. Buchanan's smile carried over to her eyes.

"If you'll excuse us now, we'll go find our seats for the performance," Mrs. Buchanan said. "Tina has been looking forward so to hearing you play, Miss Shubert." Noticing the quick flicker of Tina's gaze as it jumped to her aunt's face, Elena watched dully as the two women walked away.

"What a little twit that girl is," Jerard remarked caustically. "She doesn't make you nervous, does she?" He was looking down at Elena, his eyebrow arched arrogantly.

"Should she?" Elena asked, with the same insolent tone he was using with her.

Jerard laughed deeply. "Why don't you have dinner with me after the performance and we can talk. I think you will find what I have to say very agreeable."

Elena was looking at him now with bewilderment written all over her face. Did he mean she was not going to lose her job? She was going to be allowed to stay with the orchestra?

Her face lit up like a beacon as she gazed up at him, knowing now that everything was going to be all right. Oh, she couldn't wait until the performance was over and she could call David and tell him the good news. Although she had promised herself that she would break off any relationship with him, there was no one she would rather share this good news with than him.

Jerard, fully aware of her ebullient thoughts, skewed her with a look of disdain. As if that were not enough, he then tried to belittle her ego even further with a disparaging remark. "It's going to be a long performance, so I certainly hope you've been to the bathroom," he drawled haughtily before walking onto the stage amid reverberating applause.

Elena, trying to overlook the taunt and concentrate instead on this newfound certainty of success, walked into the footlights a few seconds behind him.

The pop of the champagne cork startled Elena out of her complacent reverie. She had been letting the normal tension of the performance drain out of her mind and body while she relaxed in one of Jerard Williams's sleek, angular chairs. His apartment was a frigid study in high-tech architecture and design. Everything in it was chrome or plastic or glass, and Elena, comparing it to her own warm decor, marveled at how anyone could live in such a cold, sterile environment. But then, she remembered, David had called her house a mausoleum, so maybe it was her own tastes that were strange.

Just thinking about David made her heart quicken. She glanced around Jerard's apartment with a frown. If only she could be with David tonight instead of with Jerard. But she knew that to toy with such possibilities was to play with a dangerous fantasy.

She had already accepted the inevitable conclusion—the recommitment of a decision made years before—that she could not have both David and her career. She had chosen her music. It was the vital core in her life. And yet, now that it appeared as if everything was beginning to settle and she was feeling more secure in her position, perhaps she could see him sometimes. She wasn't sure if she could bear the thought of not seeing him at all, ever again.

"Here you go." Jerard held out a glass of champagne for Elena. When she reached for it, circling her fingers around the fragile stem, she watched and felt with a curious remoteness as Jerard's finger brushed a seductive pattern across her hand.

If he had hoped to stir a passionate response in her, he couldn't have been farther off base. She was realistic enough to face the facts concerning her own physical impulses, and knowing beyond a shadow of a doubt that only David could make her blood quicken with fire, Elena felt a sudden wave of nausea attack her midsection. Why was she here in Jerard's apartment?

Jerard sat in a chair adjacent to her and leaned back, crossing one leg over the other at the knee.

"It's a young world, isn't it, Elena?"

Some ambiguous note in his voice as he asked that seemingly innocuous question pricked the nerves at the back of her neck.

"Especially in the field of music," he continued, without waiting for her to respond. "Fresh from the womb is the way the symphony organization wants its musicians." He reached over and ran the back of his hand leisurely up her arm.

Aware of that same clutching sensation in her stomach, Elena set her glass of untouched champagne on the coffee table and clasped her hands in her lap. "What are you saying, Jerard?" Her voice shook as much as her thoughts, and she had to clear her throat to continue. "Are you saying that I am going to be replaced? I thought—"

"What did you think?" He leaned toward her, his fiery gaze touching and searing every angle and curve of her body.

"From what you said before we went on tonight I thought that you—you had good news for me."

"Ah, but I do," he purred like a sly, self-centered cat as he lifted her limp hand, attempting to coax a sensuous heat into it with his own lifeless palms.

"As I'm sure you know, Alexi Zsarkof has found

himself out in the cold on his ass, which is fitting, since that is precisely what he made of himself.'' He lifted her hand to his thin, moist lips. ''I'm sure you are much too smart to let yourself be trammeled by that little nymph Tina Volkowski or by her overbearing aunt.''

Elena felt as if Jerard's voice were coming from a far distance, as if she were falling down into a vertical tunnel of despair from which she could not escape. Automatically her mind was beginning to cry for help in the repetition of one name over and over. *David. . . David. . . David. I need you!*

''As you may have noticed, Mrs. Buchanan thinks the sun rises and sets in me.'' Elena looked at Jerard as he said this and she noticed the complete self-absorption that was delineated by the lines of his expression. ''What I say to the board of directors becomes law. Do you understand what I'm saying, Elena?''

Elena withdrew her hand from his grasp and felt the muscles of her face sag into a state of defeat. ''In other words, Jerard,'' she began in a monotone, ''if you want me to stay on as pianist, then the board will not contradict your wish.''

He tilted his head back and sideways, smiling his domination over her with eyes that were half-lidded. ''That is absolutely correct.''

Breathing deeply, Elena glanced at her hands twisting in her lap. ''What's the catch? I mean there is a stipulation to all of this, isn't there?'' She looked at Jerard's complacent expression and wished, for one split second, that she could physically smear his arrogant nose into the floor.

"Stipulation?" Jerard rose and walked to the bar, where, in agonizing slow motion, he poured himself another glass of champagne. He turned around to smile with that same egotistical smirk. "All I expect from you is a little gratitude, that's all."

Elena was eyeing him with open suspicion now, realizing that whatever he asked of her was most likely going to be beyond distasteful and into the profoundly sickening stage.

"If I say thank you, will that be sufficient?" she asked, already knowing the answer.

Jerard chuckled unkindly before setting his glass on the counter and walking toward her with slow, deliberate paces. Bending over, he grasped Elena's upper arms and lifted her to her feet.

"That's not exactly what I had in mind." He chuckled lewdly again.

David! her mind continued to scream. *I need you!*

"I'm a lonely man in a new city," he began, stroking the shaft of her upper arms. "I need a little physical ministration, a warm, supple body next to mine." Elena stiffened as he lowered his lips to her neck.

"You are not an unforgettable beauty, Elena. I'm sure you know that. I suppose some men like their women young and virginal. But I prefer those who are more like you. A little older. A little flawed. A little frayed around the edges. And yet, there is an alluring something about you. You're very...appetizing." His mouth once again began to wander possessively across her throat as if her flesh had already become his property.

She squeezed her eyes shut in an effort to mitigate the emotional anguish. So it had come down to that in the end. Her career depended on her ability and acquiescence to sleep with a man she did not love. A man who was so detestable he made her skin crawl. A painful bubble of hysteria was lodged in her throat, allowing neither laughter nor tears to issue forth.

Whether she was able to remain a concert pianist depended nothing at all on how well she played the piano. It depended on how well she could satisfy her conductor in bed. God! What happened to the dignity of her profession? Where was the glory, the goodness, that should accompany it?

She suddenly and inexplicably wondered how many other women in the world had found themselves in this position. How many had faced this ultimate degradation to save that one dream they had carried with them all their lives.

"There is a man...." Elena felt the driving need to insert David's presence into this tawdry scene. She needed the wholesomeness of his image, his name, his affection for her, to clear away the ugliness of this situation. "He is my—"

"Elena," Jerard whispered menacingly close to her face. "I have no desire to hear of any other men in your life. I will put this as simply as I can. Get rid of them and devote all of your attention to me or you can say good-bye to your career and join Alexi in the ranks of the unemployed."

Good-bye to the dream she had harbored, nurtured, honed to a fine skill every day since she was six years old. Could she say good-bye and never look back? Would she someday regret that she did not close her eyes with Jerard and pretend that she was with someone else, with that one man who could make her feel beautiful and right?

She had never slapped anyone before, so she had no idea how much her own hand would sting from the resounding blow she administered to his cheek.

As she ran to the door, grabbing her coat from a nearby chair, she was aware that behind her Jerard was still staggering from the blow, his low voice swearing unintelligibly at her retreating figure.

Dave flipped off the television in disgust. A movie about angry worms terrorizing a small community was not exactly his idea of good entertainment. He rummaged through his music tapes and, deciding finally on a violin concerto, shoved it into his tape deck.

Stretching his back and arm muscles, he glanced at the clock. Eleven thirty. Despite his lingering anger over Elena's behavior in the lobby the other night, he couldn't help but wonder how her performance went tonight. Besides, maybe it was just as much his fault as hers. After all, he was the one who decided to take her home rather than bring her to his room.

But how much was he expected to take? One minute she acted as if she wanted nothing more than to be in his arms, and the next minute she was single-mindedly swept up in her career. She was so damned unpredictable! Maybe he should go down to the bar and try to sort out all of this.

Dave walked into the bathroom and turned on the shower. As he removed his clothes he threw them onto the heap of dirty laundry on the floor.

If only he could figure out what Elena wanted. If

he could make her realize that he didn't want to destroy her career. All he wanted was to love her and be loved in return.

He adjusted the water to warm, then stepped into the shower, tilting the spray onto his head.

He had to stop thinking about her. It was playing havoc with his work. After announcing the game last weekend, he realized for the first time how exciting this new career was going to be. Sure, he missed the action of actually playing the game and the camaraderie among the teammates afterward in the locker room. But he was beyond that stage now, and he was going to do his damnedest to make a success of this job. He wanted a renewal of his contract. And he was determined that he was going to get it!

He squeezed some shampoo onto his hair and began vigorously massaging his scalp, washing away any doubts about whether he could make it in the world of announcing.

After rinsing his hair, he soaped himself, his thoughts flying back and forth between his job security and Elena. How long was he willing to wait for her? he wondered in a fit of rebellion. What exactly did she expect from him?

After rinsing away the last of the soap, Dave turned off the shower and stepped out onto the bath mat, where he rubbed his body and hair vigorously with a towel. Rolling the towel and wrapping it around his neck, he walked to the closet and grabbed a pair of underwear and jeans. He slipped them on, then went back to the bathroom to finish drying his hair.

Before he could turn on the blow dryer, he heard a

knock at the door. He glanced at the clock. Almost midnight. Who could be visiting at this hour?

He grabbed a shirt off a hanger and slipped it on, buttoning it as quickly as possible. He didn't take the time to tuck it into his jeans as he walked across the room.

Using the towel to rub his still wet hair, he opened the door. He stared down in surprise at Elena, who looked like a lost waif in need of a hot meal.

"David?" Elena's voice was only a decibel above a sigh. Her head was bowed, but he could see the tears that glistened like liquid fire in her eyes. "Can we talk?" She looked up at his face, so wary and guarded. He had every right to feel that way. After all, he must wonder how many times she was going to lead him on.

Dave held the door open, a silent invitation for her to enter. He didn't yet trust his voice to speak. He didn't even know what he would say to her. After the tricks she had pulled with him in the past few weeks, it was bizarre even to himself to realize that he really did want her here.

"Talk?" he finally asked, lingering doubt etched in every decibel of his voice.

"Please don't make this any more difficult for me than it already is, David. I need someone to talk to." She was vaguely aware of the classical music floating from his tape player by the bed.

"Someone," he laughed bitterly. "Well, that's just great."

"Not just anyone, David. I need...you."

He turned with a cautious eye to watch her features as she looked at him. Her eyes were red-rimmed and dull, as if everything that was important in her life had suddenly dissipated.

Dave smiled tenderly and expelled the breath he had been holding since he opened the door and found her standing in the hallway. Wrapping her within the large circle of his arms, he responded gently without words.

Relaxing in the warmth and security of his arms, Elena let the sordidness of the evening drain from her. Here was where she belonged. This was the only man who could make her realize that there was more to life than her music. Because with David she felt her body to be a perfectly tuned instrument, one that he could play and stroke until within her she felt the creation of a symphonic poem, permeated with romantic intimacy, replacing entirely the need for her piano.

However, she had to talk. She had come to him because she needed his strength and guidance, his friendship.

Pulling reluctantly out of his arms, Elena placed the flat of her palm gently against his cheek. "I really did come to talk, David. I wanted to be with you. I needed to desperately."

"Okay." He stepped back to give her space and grabbed the towel that had fallen to the floor. "Listen, come into the bathroom with me while I dry my hair."

Elena followed him into the still steamy room and sat on the edge of the tub while Dave blow-dried his hair. When he finally flicked off the machine, she again spoke.

"David, even though I've come here tonight to

take advantage of your friendship, would it bother you if— Well, what I mean is…would you think I was terribly ungrateful if I said we shouldn't make love tonight?''

''Ungrateful!'' His eyes widened in surprise. ''Why on earth would you think I wanted gratitude?'' Elena walked back out into the bedroom, and Dave's eyes narrowed on her in bewilderment. ''What happened to you tonight, Elena?''

She turned away from him, hugging her arms tightly about her waist in self-protection. Walking over to the window, she flicked the curtains aside and stared broodingly down at the street below.

''I was offered a chance to keep my position with the symphony.'' She spoke in dejected tones as she watched the incessant, wearisome traffic surging through the downtown streets. ''All I had to do was sleep with my conductor.'' She turned around to catch Dave's expression, but she was disappointed. His face was blank, revealing nothing of what he thought.

He stared at her, afraid to move the muscles of his face for fear his darkening emotions would frighten her. He felt something deep within him billowing upward, a rage, a disbelief, a sorrow, something so powerful he had to keep his fists clenched at his sides to keep his brain from snapping.

He walked over to her and frowned down into her face. He wrapped his fingers around her upper arm with gentle pressure that defied the raging forces that were with him.

''You mean to tell me,'' he growled hoarsely, ''that if you don't have sex with your conductor, you will be fired?''

She shook her head dejectedly. "I don't know, David. I just don't know. He told me that—"

"When was this?" he demanded.

She glanced upward at his tightly held expression. "Tonight."

"Where?"

"At his apartment."

A shutter dropped over his expression. "I see," he stated coolly. He loosened his hold on her arms and walked away from her to sit on the edge of the bed, where he folded his hands to his lap and waited.

Realizing he didn't see anything, Elena unzipped her coat and laid it across the couch, then walked over to where Dave was sitting. Kneeling in front of him, she placed her hands on his knees. "Please be my friend and listen to me. Please!"

He smiled crookedly and expelled a short half-laugh. "It's funny. If I didn't have to fight every muscle in my body to keep from dragging you into this bed with me, I'd like nothing more than to be your friend. I even thought at one point—when you weren't very receptive to my advances—that maybe we could be just friends. But, Elena, if that's all you want me to be, I'm—I'm not really sure that I can."

Elena dropped her forehead to David's knee, relishing the feel of his large hand on the back of her head, his fingers brushing and winding slowly through her hair.

When she at last spoke, her voice was a hypnotic flow. "When I was a little girl, maybe seven or eight, I remember sitting one day at the piano, diligently practicing my scales and chords over and over again and wishing I was anywhere but at the piano.

"In my mind I saw myself as an older woman, playing those same scales before an audience. I was bored and they were bored. But suddenly this man rose out of the audience and walked onto the stage, taking my hands and lifting me from the bench."

Elena stopped talking and looked up at David, pain and sadness etched into her features. "I knew the moment he touched me that I would never play the piano again, that I would never be subjected to the tedium of those scales and those long hours of practice. Since that day that fantasy-nightmare has been with me. When I met you at the university, I was afraid that you were that man. And at that point I had invested so much of my life into my music that I couldn't give it up."

Dave waited for her to continue, and when she didn't, he asked, "And now?"

She shrugged, smiling. "I don't know...I mean you managed to shift careers quite well. Maybe I could too."

He cupped her face between his hands. "We've got each other, Elena. Even if you lose your job, you won't lose me."

"I'm not the dependent type, David."

"I never knew." He frowned seriously, but his mouth was slanted crookedly in a grin. "Look." He tilted her head up until she was forced to look at him. "I told you we were a duet. We are, Elena. We're a team. Our notes are equally important. Besides," he concluded, "you can write music for a living. You'll become the next Marvin Hamlisch and we'll make a fortune."

Elena laughed easily now, relieved that the weight

of the demoralizing evening had been lifted from her shoulders. She stood up, feeling much lighter and more content than she had in a long time.

With a pert confidence that surprised them both, Elena climbed onto the bed with Dave, propped up the pillows against the headboard, and leaned back.

Smiling in pleasant surprise, Dave reclined on his side, holding up his torso with his elbow.

"Now, you want to talk about what happened at Alexi Zsarkof's tonight?"

"It wasn't Alexi. It was Jerard Williams." She glanced at Dave and noticed him visibly stiffen.

"I could tell you were attracted to him," Dave's mouth tightened as he thought back to that night in the hotel lobby.

"I wasn't attracted to him," Elena emphasized. "I was attracted to the image. He's a famous conductor. But the man inside is a cold, unfeeling animal. And, David, the only reason I went to his apartment was because he said he had some good news to tell me. He's replaced Alexi as conductor and I wanted to establish a good working relationship with him. I had no idea that—" Her voice broke as she recalled Jerard's crude proposition.

"He didn't hurt you, did he?" Dave berated himself for not thinking of that before now, and his blood began to boil with anger over the possibility.

"No," she quickly reassured him. "He didn't. He—" She smiled weakly. "Do you think I'm attractive, David? I'm not fishing for idle compliments," she asserted in a rush when she caught the surprised flicker in his eyes. "I mean, I know I'm...sort of attractive, but are you attracted to me because I'm frayed around the edges?''

"Frayed around the edges!" Dave's mouth was gaping wide and his eyes were lit with puzzled amusement. In one swift motion he grasped her waist and roughly jerked her body until she was lying on her back next to him. He placed a knee over her thighs and held her arms above her head with one hand.

Then his inquiring but reverent gaze began a long, slow perusal of her oval face and slim neck; her round breasts, rising in agitation under the lacy, blue silk blouse; her waist, dipping in before it flared gently into curving hips; her stomach, flat beneath the waistband of her skirt.

His gaze traveled lower and held steady, seeing through the gray flannel skirt to what lay waiting beneath, wanting to stroke the creamy flesh of her inner thighs with fingertips that almost throbbed with desire.

"Frayed around the edges," he whispered in disgust. "You are like a tiny golden flower."

"On a vine with a thousand other tiny golden flowers," she murmured nervously, embarrassed and at the same time thrilled by Dave's intense examination of her.

Dave watched the flush that crept across her face, and smiled softly. "But you are the one with the sweetest fragrance, the one the bees return to time and time again because they know they will never find a flower as bountiful with nectar as you."

Dave released her arms and lowered his body until he was partially covering her. "This is one bee who will never look anywhere else," he whispered huskily.

Elena ran her hand along the side of his neck, pushing her fingers into the unruly hair above his ears.

"Didn't you fall in love with anyone in the past twelve years, David?" Elena's other hand reached up and her fingers were stroking the hair on the opposite side of his head. "Wasn't there. . .someone who was special?" She held her breath, wanting yet not wanting to know if any other woman had known the thrill of his arms and body.

"I found quite a few warm bodies," he admitted. "But the only special woman was the one in my dreams, the eighteen-year-old girl I had carried in my memory since college." As he gazed lovingly at her she had no doubt as to who that girl was. "What about you?"

"I almost got married once." She felt a stab of pain as she watched the hurt shoot across Dave's eyes. "It's not really as serious as it sounds. It was after I transferred to the university here. I met a boy in my music theory class. He was looking for a music major to marry so that he and she could become another Ferante and Teicher. I guess he thought I was the one."

"But you said you almost married him." He hesitated over the words, not wanting to hear of her love for another man.

"He made it sound like the right thing to do."

"Did you love him?"

"No, David, I didn't love him. After I left you, I promised myself I wouldn't love again. Ever. And I haven't."

Dave pulled her body up tighter against his hips

and dipped his head down to nibble along the fluttering pulse in her neck.

She loved the feel of his body in her arms. His muscles were taut and rippling beneath his skin. The weight of his body filled her with a sense of possession, his strength flowing into every pore of her body. He was heavier than he was at twenty, but the weight was distributed not into flab but into muscles of steel. He must have been a formidable football player, she found herself thinking.

"Do you miss playing football, David?" Elena's mouth was on his hair, and as she spoke, her breath ran warm and fleeting across his scalp.

He raised his head to look at her, but his thoughts were pulling at the good memories of years past. "Sometimes I really do. Every once in a while I get this ache in my gut, like I've got to get out there on the field and play. Maybe you feel this when you're on stage. But it's like an incredible flow of adrenaline surging through your body. You can't help but feel alive. I thrived on the competition, the roughness, the dedication. And—" he looked a little sheepish "—I must admit that I did enjoy the crowd response. The knowledge that everyone is up there in those stands watching you is pretty heady stuff."

"I know exactly what you mean," Elena agreed. "I've felt that same way on stage."

"But I know too that I couldn't have kept on playing. I reached my limit. I suppose everyone has these fleeting moments of greatness sometime in their lives, but they can't last forever. Most of the time we plod along on a pretty even keel. It's funny, but sometimes I wish we didn't have so many choices to make in our lives. Don't you think it was easier for people during our grandparents' day and age when life was more patterned?''

''I don't know. Maybe if you don't have any choices to make, you can't ever aspire to greatness. Wasn't it Browning who said 'A man's reach should exceed his grasp, or what's a heaven for'?''

Dave rolled over onto his back, pulling Elena on top of him. ''Tell me I'm not exceeding my grasp with you, Elena.''

Elena would have told him. She would have filled the air with the words that described how she felt about him. But before she got a chance, his hands were moving under her blouse, sweeping across the bare expanse of her back. She could feel the hard raptures of his body beneath her thighs as his arms held her tightly, molding her pliant flesh to his.

One hand came up and pulled her face down to meet his. Her lips met his warm persuasive mouth and her blood swept into a tidal wave of desire as his tongue parted her lips and began to savor the moist interior of her mouth.

Abandoning her mouth for a moment, Dave trailed kisses across her cheek and throat, his tongue darting along the sensitive veins of her neck.

''How serious were you about not wanting to make love?'' he whispered huskily into her ear, sending a shiver of longing across her skin.

''Did I say that?'' Her voice quavered breathlessly as Dave's hand moved upward beneath the silk blouse, curving under the gentle swell of her breast. She opened her mouth to respond, but his thumb swept across the tip, stiffening it to an erect and sensitive peak and sending a shudder of delight through her. Her thoughts were lost, wandering aimlessly amid a forest of sensation, too enraptured to bother searching for a way out.

His hand was on the top button of her blouse, teasing her with his intention to free it from its hole. "Elena?" His breath stroked her face. "Is this what you want?"

She tried to will her blouse open under his hands, wanted to press her flesh against him until they were one. "I want you, David. I want to make love with you."

The button slipped easily through the hole. Soon the others followed and Dave once again rolled her over onto her back. His eyes were trained on the alabaster flesh of her breasts and stomach that were now exposed to him.

His gaze worshiped her skin as it followed his hand in exploration.

Elena felt as if her body could take flight, as if David were finally unshackling the bonds that had held her away from him for so long.

He continued to strum her flesh as if she were a delicate harp, his fingers brushing lightly across the mounds of her breasts, striking just the right chords to make her nerves sing.

She lifted her palms to his face and began a slow exploration of his strong features, his muscular neck and shoulders, down his arms until her hands were atop his.

For a moment he stopped caressing her, taking her hands in his and gripping them tightly. He lifted them to his lips, brushing a tender kiss across her knuckles, before he placed her arms out to the side of her body and began, once again, to awaken her flesh to untold pleasures.

She couldn't lie still for long. Her own hands shook with the need to touch him as he was touching her. He dropped the tempo of his caresses to adagio, slow, tranquil brush strokes, as he watched, mesmerized by her hands lifting to his shirt, her fingers trembling at the top button.

"Let me help you."

"I can't seem to make my fingers work right," she apologized.

Dave took the hand that was shaking so badly, and slowly and deliberately kissed each finger. "Don't apologize. And don't be in too much of a hurry. We've got the whole night ahead of us to play this symphony."

Chapter Eight

Elena had never felt so utterly alive with exquisite sensations as she did in this moment. Touches of sweet harmony fell across her skin and her fingers played soft refrains on David's chest and stomach and back.

Steady heat rose in waves from their bodies. His large hands were molding her body—her breasts, her waist, her hips. His fingers stroked her stomach, drawing tantalizing circles of desire on her flesh.

Slowly easing down the zipper of her skirt, Elena lifted her body so that David could slide it off her hips, pushing it down past her ankles and onto the floor. Not waiting for her trembling fingers to perform the same task for him, he stood and quickly removed his pants and his already unbuttoned shirt.

Elena marveled at the strength and virility of his body, wanting more than anything to be possessed by him and, in turn, to possess him.

Dave lowered himself to the bed, covering her naked flesh with his own. Elena's mouth dipped down to scatter featherlike kisses across his bare chest. His lips buried into the throbbing pulse at her neck.

They were engulfed in symphonic ecstasy, pressing skin to skin, wrapping themselves in the moist heat from their bodies as it rose and clung to the air around them, enveloping them in a vapor of sensuality.

Dave's hands began a thorough exploration of the secret depths of her body, causing Elena to tremble and gasp with turbulent desire.

"David, please!" she cried, urging her body upward into the curve of his.

His fingers slowed, moving upward to cover her breasts and tease her almost beyond endurance. His mouth covered one breast, his tongue circling the tip and pulling it gently into the warm, moist recesses of his mouth. "Don't make me hurry with you, Elena," he breathed against her breast. "Let me love you the way you should be, slowly and carefully."

"I don't think I can wait!" she implored. "I need you so!"

Dave ran his fingers through her hair, massaging her scalp with tender strokes. "You're going to have to wait," he growled softly in her ear, his tongue flicking out to replace his voice. "I'm going to take you on a long, slow journey, and I have no intention of taking any detours or shortcuts."

Elena's hands clutched at his back, her fingers digging into the muscles that rippled beneath his flesh. "Yes...oh, yes," she murmured. "Take me with you."

As her hands glided down to his waist and onto his hips, she urged her fingers into his flesh, pressing him more tightly against her. And she thrilled to the low moan that was wrenched from his throat.

His tongue began a foray across her skin, stopping to savor the delight of her breasts before traveling down across her stomach.

In lento timing his tongue strummed her sensitive skin; each tremulant tone that he invoked within her was sustained legatissimo, prolonging her delicious agony.

Her hands were in his hair, tugging the strands between clutching fingers as he drove her beyond the edge of desire into the realm of delirium.

She felt the pressure in her body mount, expanding and dilating into a vibrating force that could not be stopped. Her entire physical being was like a swaying bridge trapped in a harmonic motion that had complete control over her.

Dave knew he couldn't hold off much longer. He wanted to prolong her enjoyment forever. He never wanted to stop tasting and touching her. But her hands were all over him, pulling and groping for him. And, her desire for him invoked in his body and soul an uncontrollable need for her.

Shifting his body upward, he finally succumbed to the physical union they both craved so desperately. The warmth of her flesh around him surged through his bloodstream, carrying him to an elevation he had never reached before.

Grasping both of her hands, he held them against the bed to the side of her head. Their fingers intertwined, squeezing rhythmically to the timing of their undulating bodies.

As they moved, Dave looked down upon Elena's face. Her facial muscles were tight and she was watching him, her eyes closing now and then, reflecting the mounting urgency between them.

She was being stroked into deafening crescendo, the music of passion swelling until the throbbing sounds consumed her mind and body.

"I love you, Elena," Dave whispered, before clenching his eyes and jaw tightly as the penetration of body and mind coincided.

As explosive, erupting pleasure seized their bodies, their entwined fingers were clasped in an almost painful grip, a visible manifestation of the mystical union between physical and spiritual that had just taken place.

It was a long time before either of them moved. Loosening his fingers from her still tight grasp, Dave brushed the wet hair back from her face. Little drops of perspiration clung to her skin and he slowly began to kiss them away.

Elena lay very still. She couldn't have moved if she tried. Something that had lain dormant in her for so long had finally exploded and she knew she would never be the same. Something profoundly spiritual was happening to her and it was with breathless wonder that she realized there was no music in the world that could describe the beauty of what she felt.

Rolling to the side, Dave pulled her head onto his chest. As he stroked her hair he could sense a communication between them that needed few words.

"Whatever happens, Elena, we've got each other," Dave whispered against her hair. He knew by her breathing that she was asleep, but he wanted the words in the air.

After a few moments he too let sleep overtake him, the half-smile that played around his lips reflecting the sense of peace he now knew.

Elena awoke and glanced at Dave's clock on the nightstand. Seven thirty. The curtains were closed, but a slim shaft of early morning light pierced the crack between the draperies. She looked over at Dave sleeping so contentedly next to her, and she smiled. His brown hair was tousled against the pillow and one arm was thrown above his head. The sheet and blanket had fallen down past his waist, and Elena let her gaze wander slowly over the contours of his body.

In the half light his skin glowed brown and healthy. The sturdy muscles across his broad chest were taut and hard. Brown hair was tufted on his chest, trailing down toward his stomach. His waist was trim, his stomach flat, attesting to the fact that exercise was still a way of life for him.

Her gaze lingered at the spot on his abdomen where the sheet began. She had never known such fulfillment as David had shown her. For twelve years she had carried the intimation of what it would be like to make love to him. Her eyes flickered knowingly. Now she knew.

When her gaze lifted to his face, she was startled to see that he was watching her.

"Good morning." He smiled. "Don't let me interrupt your inspection."

Elena had the grace to blush, and even in the dimly lit room Dave could see the pink flush that crept up her cheeks. He pulled her down on top of him, only the thin sheet separating their naked bodies.

A new wave of heat surged through Elena's body, and she felt herself drawn once again into the mystic chambers of her physical desire for this man.

"I have to practice," she moaned unconvincingly, tilting her head back to give Dave's mouth better access to her neck and running her fingers through his hair.

"I'll be your piano," he breathed huskily against her throat. "You can practice your finger exercises on me as long as you like."

The restaurant seemed to glint with opulence. An enormous gold and crystal chandelier glittered above the patrons' heads. Each table was covered with a linen cloth, a single long-stemmed rose in the center adding understated elegance to the setting. Haviland china and Waterford crystal provided the canvas for creative continental cuisine.

Eunice Buchanan tipped her glass of white wine, sipping delicately as she scanned the restaurant for anyone noteworthy. "My dear," she soothed, "it's only a matter of time. You must be patient."

"I'm tired of being patient." Tina thrust her lower lip into a pout, her eyes flashing with the temper of a four-year-old. "I want to play now!"

"Don't be tiresome, Tina. These things have to be handled delicately."

"I don't see why you don't just fire her."

"For what reason?" Eunice Buchanan's patience was wearing thin with this sniveling child. Tina had always been overindulged, making her an added burden for Eunice, who didn't even like children. But she was the daughter of her only sister and she had promised to help get her started in this business.

"Why can't you say I play better than her?" Tina's voice was growing more like a whine by the minute.

"Because you don't." Eunice Buchanan took a certain amount of delight in watching Tina flinch.

"Not yet, anyway. Elena Shubert has years of experience behind her that you do not have. If Jerard Williams asked you what you could play on twenty-four-hour notice, what could you tell him?"

Tina's chin jutted forward defensively. "My repertoire may not be as large as hers, but I play like an angel."

Eunice Buchanan stared blankly at her niece.

"I want her out!" Tina almost shouted when her aunt ignored her.

"Do shut up, Tina. You're giving me a headache." Eunice glanced up at the doorway of the restaurant as the executive director of the symphony walked toward them. "Ah, here is Richard Flanders. Now, keep your mouth shut and try to look demure. We're going to need him."

Eunice Buchanan held out her hand to Richard, trite social drivel gushing from her bright red lips.

Richard smiled at the influential board member, reminding himself that, however hard it might be, he must be nice to the woman. After all, his position with the symphony was only as permanent as the Board of Directors' fondness for him. As his gaze swept to Tina she was smiling coquettishly but he couldn't help but notice that her eyes held the look of anything but virginal innocence.

He knew already the purpose of this little get-together. Eunice wanted him to fire Elena Shubert so that her niece could become the orchestra's pianist. Trying to ignore the bad taste this particular action left in his mouth, Richard Flanders sat down to listen to the two determined women.

As the dessert dishes were carried off by an attentive waiter, Eunice Buchanan's and Tina Volkowski's faces held identical expressions of bovine contentedness. They had chewed on Richard Flanders for over an hour and they now had him right where they wanted him.

"I suppose a two-piano concert could be a drawing card for the symphony," Richard agreed hesitantly.

"Of course it would." Eunice was not going to give him a moment to reconsider.

"I doubt if Elena Shubert will be very enthusiastic about this." He frowned, wondering if he could delegate to the conductor the task of informing her.

"Well, then, it's settled!" Eunice dropped her linen napkin onto the table, signaling an end to the conversation. "Jerard can decide what they will play. We'll do it on Friday night."

"The program is already at the printer's," Richard hedged.

"Well, it will just have to be changed, won't it?"

"I guess so," he replied, pulling out a stack of bills to pay for the sizable check.

Eunice Buchanan's hand fluttered down over Richard's. "This is my treat, Richard darling," she said, sliding the check from his fingers.

"Well—" he stood to go, relieved that at least his wallet had been spared from the woman's clutches "—it's been...interesting, ladies. Good day." His mouth curved into a final tired smile before he walked away.

Eunice tipped her glass to Tina, a conspiratorial smile twisting her mouth sideways. All in all, it had been an extraordinarily successful luncheon.

"I don't see why I have to play with her," Tina whined. "I don't see why he doesn't just fire her and get it over with. I want to perform by myself. I want—"

"Shut up, Tina," Eunice sighed as she began to rub her throbbing temples.

Elena took out the loaf of bread, then stared at the vast array of food that was in her refrigerator. David had gone wild at the grocery store the other day and she had no idea how she would ever eat all of this. She pulled open the meat bin and lifted a pack of bologna. Scowling at the meat, she opened the package and grasped a thin slice between her fingers.

Dropping it quickly onto the bread as if it were alive, she placed the other slice of bread on top and carried it on a paper plate to the table.

As she munched on the sandwich she thought about David. She had only left his room two hours ago, and already she missed him terribly. What was he doing now? she wondered. Was he thinking about her? About last night? About this morning?

She had guessed, at eighteen, that loving David would totally consume her. She believed that once she had felt his possession, she would never be able to loosen the ties that would bind her to him. Now she knew that, at eighteen years old, she had been one hundred percent correct.

Her thoughts were of him every minute and she found it extremely difficult to concentrate on the music for the next performance. She was simply going to have to learn how to juggle her career and her relationship with David. She could do it. She knew that now. For the first time in her life she felt she could have it all.

Dave heard the phone ringing as he turned the key in his door. He had just spent a frustrating three hours with a realtor who, mistakenly assuming that all football players were millionaires, insisted on showing him houses that were far beyond his financial reach.

Tossing his coat and briefcase onto the bed, he grabbed the receiver.

"Hello?"

"Dave? Jerry Monroe here. I've been trying to get a hold of you for two hours. Don't tell me you're already out of money and looking for a second job."

Dave's chuckle was devoid of amusement. How gullible people were. They actually believed the media hype about all pro athletes swimming in money. He could deny it, but what was the use? People would believe what they wanted to believe.

"Listen," Jerry was saying. "A group of us have worked up a trip to Vail next week. A guy I know has a condo there and we can stay for free. What do you say? Kristin Langley is going," he snickered nastily. "She always did have the hots for you, Atwell."

"I don't think so, Jerry. I've got a lot going right now. Besides—" He started to tell Jerry about Elena, but at the last second decided against it, realizing that Jerry would probably make some crude or off-color remark, thus ending their friendship on the spot. "I've got to go to New York next week," he said instead.

"Well, it's your loss. If you don't keep Kristin

warm at night, she'll have to find somebody else."

"Yeah, well, thanks anyway."

"Okay, see you later. If you change your mind, give me a call."

"I'll do that." Dave hung up the phone with a sigh of relief. A few weeks ago if he had received an invitation like that, he would have immediately started packing his bags. But now his thoughts were only of Elena. The thought of warming any other woman's body, including the well-endowed Kristin Langley's, left his blood as cold as ice.

Chapter Nine

By the time Elena walked to rehearsal, the temperature had risen into the fifties. The sun was shining brightly and the air hinted of spring. It had been a long winter and warmer days couldn't come too soon for her.

The only dark cloud hanging over her was the one that cast Jerard Williams's shadow. Although she realized the power of the famous maestro, she refused to let him intimidate her. She had been involved in the music world for too many years to let his attitude crush her spirit. She would fight to the end for her right to play with this orchestra. If she lost the fight, she at least had David to help her through it. The two of them together were invincible!

But how was Jerard going to act toward her today? After all, she did slap his face. What would his attitude be like?

Elena climbed the steps of the music hall, the wooden handle of her brown leather music case clutched in her left hand. Today they would be going over the Dvořák and then probably the two Sibelius pieces they would play for the contemporary composer series.

After entering the wide double doors, she crossed the marble-tiled foyer and opened a door that led to a long, narrow hallway. Walking its length, she passed practice rooms, dressing rooms, and numerous storage closets. As she entered the wings many of the musicians were already there, setting up their stands and sheet music and visiting with each other before rehearsal began.

She saw Jerard standing across the room, and with an expression that was chiseled from ice he nodded crisply to her. Elena sighed with relief. He may be angry, she decided, but at least he was going to be professional enough to carry on a business relationship without causing a melodramatic scene.

Elena strode to the glossy black Steinway and began setting up her sheet music. A commotion on the right wing suddenly drew her attention. Several stagehands were pushing another piano onto the stage. When they halted, with the instrument only a few feet in front of Elena's piano, she began to frown.

Turning around to see where Jerard was so that he could explain this unseemly hullabaloo, she watched him walk toward her with Tina Volkowski at his side. As Elena's gaze shifted to the girl, she noticed an ugly, supercilious smile plastered across the other pianist's face.

Elena felt a chill slide ominously through her bloodstream. What was going on? What on earth was happening here?

She stared at Jerard for the answer, her expression blank as she tried to hide her anxiety. "The directors have decided that it would be a good idea to have a two-piano concert." Though his voice was cool and detached, Elena thought she detected a hint of distaste for this arrangement. "You and Tina will be playing the concerto for two pianos on Friday."

"Which concerto?" Elena's voice was surprisingly strong and calm, concealing the inner emotional turmoil that was turning her stomach upside down.

"This." He handed each of them sheet music of a Mozart concerto for two pianos. "Please make sure you know your parts." With that, Jerard turned away from the two women and moved to his podium.

Elena and Tina stared at each other for one long, hostile moment, neither one wanting to be the first to speak. Jerard settled the question for them by turning around, impatiently growling, "Tina, would you please sit down so that we can rehearse."

Flustered and embarrassed that she was singled out in front of the orchestra, Tina rushed to the piano and sat down.

Jerard was still looking at Elena, and she glared at him with anger and hurt. His behavior toward her the other night had been disgusting enough, but if bringing Tina into the orchestra was his way of paying her back, it was unforgivable.

Jerard's shoulder lifted in a slight upward shrug, and suddenly Elena knew that he had had nothing to do with this turn of events. Beyond that, his expression showed clearly that he was not happy about it either.

Elena sighed with relief. At least it looked as if that tawdry episode could be put behind them where it belonged and they could interact with each other as conductor and musician.

Jerard turned back to his music and picked up the

baton. Breathing deeply, he tried to erase the image of the two women from his mind. He had misjudged Elena Shubert, that was for sure. He had erroneously believed that she would do anything to save her career, but she had made it clear the other night that there were limits. He was grateful that at least she wasn't going to act like a child over the incident.

Tina Volkowski, on the other hand, would probably be an easy mark. He already knew she would do anything at all to weasel her way into this symphony. The problem was whether he could put up with her rotten temperament. Well, perhaps this two-piano performance would show what she could do as a pianist. If she couldn't cut it here, he wouldn't even speculate about what she could do in other areas.

He closed his eyes and massaged his neck to dismiss the problem from his mind. Rapping his baton against the podium, he began his first lecture of the day.

Elena practiced the Dvořák with the orchestra for over an hour and a half before Jerard turned his attention back to the two pianists and their piece.

"Now, then, Elena, you will play first piano. Tina, you, of course, will play second." He was aware of Tina's peevish expression, and it amused him. How typically childish of her not to want to play accompaniment. "Please practice," he continued without pause, "because I expect this to be performed without a flaw."

"Are there practice rooms available?" Elena asked, already resigned to the fact that she must play with Tina. She had known for some time that she had competition, so it was just as well that it had finally come out into the open where she could deal with it.

"The stage is not being used this afternoon, so the two of you may remain here to practice."

As the musicians filed off stage Elena was aware of their curious stares, some sympathetic, some totally apathetic. She sat stiffly on the piano bench, afraid that if she moved it might be to throttle that simpleminded girl who sat at the other piano.

Tina was the first to move. She stood and walked over to Elena's piano, leaning against its body with casual disrespect for the beautiful wood grain.

"So." She glanced lovingly at her own hands. "How did you trick Jerard into letting you play primo?"

Elena glared at the girl with open dislike. "Don't forget, little girl, that I am the pianist with this orchestra. You're merely a secondary player."

Not for long, Tina reflected with an ugly twist of her mouth. Not for long.

"Now, let's get started," Elena commanded. "I play these first six measures and then you come in with the orchestra. Here is the tempo." Even though Elena had not played this piece for years, the notes automatically flowed from her fingers. She began playing the first few bars, counting aloud for Tina's benefit. "Three and four... and one and two... and three and... I hold here and then you come in on the fourth beat."

"Well," Tina added sourly as she walked back to her piano. "I certainly hope they tune and voice your middle register before the performance. Your tones sound hideous."

Elena rolled her eyes and bit back all the things she

would like to say to Tina. Jerard was right; she was a twit. But at least Tina had not completely replaced Elena. There was hope yet.

They went over the piece time and time again and Elena tried with all her might to retain her patience. Tina played extremely well, but she refused to follow instructions and constantly improvised when she couldn't get the timing correct.

By the time they had finished practicing, tempers were short and Elena couldn't get away from her fast enough. As she closed her music and stood, she noticed out of the corner of her eye that someone was in the audience watching them. As she focused on the figure walking toward her, she smiled.

"How long have you been here, David?"

"A while. I couldn't wait until tonight to see you."

Elena blushed and began shoving her papers into the satchel.

Tina remained seated on her bench, her hand poised in midair with the sheet music grasped between her fingers. Her eyes swept down the man's body with lascivious intent. Men were her specialty, and older men had always held a particular fascination for her. She peered over the top of her piano as he leaned over to kiss Elena. A flash of jealousy sparked through her veins, adding to the hate she already felt for Elena Shubert.

How could he care about Elena? She was a has-been. Suddenly a wonderful idea trickled into the circuitry of Tina's brain. Her eyes narrowed to tiny slits as she began to calculate her chances. Before the concert was over, Elena Shubert was going to have lost this game. Not only would Tina have Elena's spot with the orchestra, but she was going to have her man too.

An ugly, devious smile curled her upper lip as she continued to stare at Elena and David whispering to each other so lovingly.

"Let's go get some dinner," Dave suggested as they left the music hall.

"David, there's enough food in my refrigerator to feed us for a year," Elena reminded him.

"No, I mean let's go somewhere different. I realized this morning that I've never even taken you to a nice restaurant."

"Ah-ha," she laughed. "Feeling guilty because you ravished me without first wining and dining me, aren't you?"

"You've got to be kidding!" he exclaimed. "If it's a case of who ravished whom, then you owe me the dinner."

"Is that so?"

He wrapped his arm around her waist, nuzzling the top of her head with his mouth. "That is so."

She felt warmth surging through her body as she leaned into David's strong frame. How had she ever gotten along without him? she wondered with amazement. It was now so obvious to her that they really did belong together. That they had always belonged together.

"Where do you want to eat, then?" she asked as he opened the car door for her.

"Do you like Italian?"

"Love it."

"I know a place on the east side of town that has the best linguini with clam sauce I've ever tasted."

"Sounds wonderful, but can I change clothes first?" She noticed the nice slacks and shirt he was wearing, then compared them with her own attire of jeans and cotton print blouse.

"Sure. We'll stop by your house, but we've got to hurry. I made a reservation for seven. And, by the way, Armando's is a very romantic place."

"Talk about presumptuous!" she laughed.

When Dave stopped the car at her house, she didn't wait for him to open her door. She jumped from the passenger side and ran up the stoop to the front door.

"Now I know what to say to make you move," Dave called after her.

"What is that?" She turned around to look at him as she turned the key.

"Linguini and clam sauce."

She laughed lightly, knowing the real key words to make her hurry were "romantic place."

"There may be some wine in one of the cupboards," she called down to him as she quickly climbed the stairs to the loft.

Dave left on his coat while he strolled into the kitchen and pulled open every cabinet. There was no wine. Shaking his head in mock disgust, he opened the refrigerator and poured himself a glass of milk. "Borden's 1983. A very good year." He downed the tall glass of milk in one gulp.

Elena rustled through her closet, pulling one thing after another off the clothes rod looking for something suitable to wear. Finally deciding on a simple velvet skirt and blouse, she laid the outfit across her bed, then went into the bathroom to wash. Leaving her thick hair tied at the back of her head in a ponytail, she wrapped it in a bun, then brushed her teeth and washed her face. What she really wanted to do was take a bath, but David probably wouldn't want to wait that long. She looked longingly at the tub, trying to decide. Oh, pooh! David could just wait.

She ran hot water into the tub, adding just enough cold water to keep herself from boiling alive. After removing her jeans, smock, panties, and bra, she dumped several capfuls of fragrant oil into the water, then cautiously dipped a small narrow foot into the steaming water.

Leaning back against the rim, she felt the tension of her day with Tina rising upward with the steamy vapor. She closed her eyes and drifted into pleasant thoughts about the evening ahead.

Dave strolled through the kitchen, the living room, back to the kitchen. He looked out the windows. He could hear water running. How much water did she need to wash her face? he wondered impatiently.

As he walked back into the living room, the scent of honeysuckle drifted down the stairs, winding around the banister and tickling the end of his nose. Was she taking a bath? His pulse began to quicken with the thought.

He stood in the middle of the living room floor, shifting indecisively from one foot to the other. Finally he removed his coat and tossed it carelessly on the couch.

Hesitantly he placed one foot on the bottom step. Very slowly he lifted his other foot to join the first. The smell of that fragrance was as intoxicating to him as any wine. Just the hint of it in the air sent his mind reeling with powerful longings for her.

The blood began to bound turbulently through his veins as he moved up the stairs, farther into the nebulous haze of honeysuckle and need.

Elena opened her eyes when a large shadow fell between her eyelids and the ceiling light. She stared at Dave towering over her and felt an incurable weakness flood through her limbs. She was mesmerized by his presence so intimately near, and she sensed that he was equally spellbound by her.

As if it were happening before her eyes in slow motion, she watched him unbutton his blue shirt, pulling the tail from beneath the waistband of his gray slacks. His eyes never left her face as he unfastened the slacks and let them drop to the floor, followed immediately by his underwear.

Elena's eyes moved from his face down the length of his muscular body, her breath quickening with each inch her gaze dropped. She wanted to reach out and stroke him, but her hand felt as if it were paralyzed.

Dave stepped into the tub and tried to wedge himself in the small space with Elena. Never taking their eyes from each other, they both laughed lightly at their cramped quarters.

"This tub ain't big enough for the two of us, pardner." David's voice was breathless and low.

Grasping Elena underneath her arms, he lifted her easily on top of him. He stretched his legs out, so she was now lying along the length of him, every tense muscle of his body ingraining itself into her flesh.

Pulling Elena's head down onto his shoulder, he stroked her back and hips and thighs. With each movement of their hands or bodies the water swirled in contentment around them.

Elena lifted her head and looked at Dave with wonder. She had never taken a bath with a man before and the raw sensuality of it excited every nerve fiber along her spine.

"What about the linguini?" Her voice was as quick and breathless as a tiny grace note.

"Linguini?" His hands had moved to her breasts, his fingers gently rubbing the peaks back and forth.

"You remember," she half-moaned, half-choked on the words. "With clam sauce?"

"Sounds delicious," he murmured abstractly as he pulled Elena's head down so that he could nuzzle her throat with his mouth. The nape of her neck was damp, and little wisps of hair now hung wetly against her back.

Dave lifted his left hand from her back, running his hand along the tiled shower wall until his fingers landed on a bar of soap. He dipped the soap into the water, then slowly and methodically began smoothing it down Elena's back and hips, his other hand rubbing it into a slick lather.

Stirred beyond the point of excitement, Elena flicked her tongue along his throat, drinking in the moistened flavor of his skin. Her fingers were winding through the strains of wet hair at the back of his neck.

"God, you smell so good, Elena. That honeysuckle scent has haunted me for so many years."

As she lifted her mouth onto his, she felt the sweeping blaze of his tongue immediately thrust inside her mouth, stroking her own tongue until it responded. Flames of fire leaped and curled through her veins, spiraling higher and higher through her bloodstream.

Dave lifted her smaller body higher onto him, parting her thighs as he did so. She moaned softly as she felt him slide slowly into her, the liquid touch of the water and the fiery caress of his hands grazing every square inch of her body.

The soap slipped from Dave's fingers as his hands suddenly clutched her waist. Elena continued to watch the play of emotions that tightened the muscles of his face. Abruptly he stopped thrusting against her, closing his eyes and clenching his jaw tightly. He was trying to restrain the release his body was craving so badly, delaying the inevitable end for as long as he could.

When he again was able to open his eyes, Elena marveled at his control. The indescribable heat that was building inside of her was something she could not have suppressed no matter how hard she might try.

Her fingers still grasped the hair at the nape of his neck and she began to move her hips against him, unable to stop the progressive flow of sexual union.

Dave joined her, digging his fingers into her hips, pulling her harder against him as he once again let the powerful urges take over. He watched Elena, want-

ing to see every trace of passion that flickered across
her face. Her lips glistened where her moist tongue
flicked across them. Her eyes were glazed with the
ever increasing intensity of her concentration. He
thrust harder against her as his gaze lowered to the
throbbing pulse in her neck.

As Elena stared at David she felt his breath so
warm and urgent against her neck. Suddenly she saw
nothing at all. Something exploded within her and
she was aware only of the dazzling lights that danced
in front of her eyes, blinding her to all but the rapturous thrill of her body so perfectly united with
David's.

Dave moaned as he felt the pulsating climax within
Elena's body. He relished in the throbbing beat of
her body as it engulfed him. And then he closed his
eyes and let the same release wash over him.

When Elena felt the warm explosion within her,
she collapsed onto Dave's chest, her ears pounding
with the sound of their hearts beating in rapid pres-
tissimo, ever so slowly decreasing to the steadier rate
of ritenuto.

After several minutes Dave's mouth moved against
her temple, kissing her almost reverently. "That was
the best linguini I've ever had." He squeezed the
flesh of her hips with gentle fingers.

"The clam sauce was out of this world," she coun-
tered, spreading soft kisses across his shoulder.

"Remind me to take you there again sometime."

A low growl rumbled between their stomachs.

"I will," she laughed. "Probably in about fifteen
minutes." She sighed, too weak to move. "Oh,
David. I've never felt so wonderful in my life."

"Yes, I know. A bath always makes you feel like a new person."

She shivered against him. "Are you cold?" The water was now tepid at best.

"Frozen, but I was too dazed to figure that out."

As they climbed from the tub Dave kept his arm protectively around Elena's waist. He grabbed a large royal-blue towel and draped it around her shoulders, drying her body as slowly and carefully as he would a child's. When he had finished drying her, he wrapped it around her body, knotting it between her breasts.

Then he took another towel and began drying himself. Elena leaned against the bathroom wall, weak with her love for this man.

"Have I ever told you I love you, David?"

"No." He rolled the towel and draped it around his neck while he watched her carefully.

"I love you."

Dave stepped to her, wrapping the rolled towel around her neck and pulling her up against him.

"I love you too." He tilted her chin upward, kissing her lovingly with still warm, damp lips. "A perfect duet that's destined to play for a long, long time."

Elena rested her palms on David's chest. She had never dreamed that it could be possible to have both David and her music career. But now he had awakened her to a brand-new symphony. One that held the delight of endless variations and possibilities. A sensuous rhapsody that would play on and on.

Though they were an hour late for their reservations, Armando's was everything Dave described it to be: romantic atmosphere and delicious food. The walls were lined with wooden wine racks, displaying a choice array of heady nectars. Subdued lighting from suspended antique candelabra cast soft rosy shadows on the ceiling and floor. Each table was secluded from the others by luxuriant ornamental plants. Red tablecloths were draped with casual elegance over each table to the floor and bronze place settings reflected the gentle glow of the room.

"You look lovely." Dave smiled at Elena, thinking to himself that lovely was totally inadequate to describe how she enhanced this setting.

She was wearing a royal-blue panne velvet skirt with a hand-painted silk blouse of a much paler blue. Around her neck she wore a cameo necklace that hung on a velvet ribbon to match her skirt. On the third finger of her right hand was a small emerald that her father had given her the day she won her first professional piano competition. Her cashmere coat was draped neatly behind her on the chair.

"I like your hair that way." She had looped it at the back of her head, a silken cord weaving through the chignon. Wavy tendrils hung loose at the nape of her neck and at her temples.

"You look wonderful yourself," she admitted, openly admiring his steady, clean-shaved face, his gentle pale green eyes caressing her with every glance.

"Well, I'm afraid my shirt and slacks got a little wrinkled on your bathroom floor. Tomorrow I'm definitely buying you an iron."

"You don't expect me to stay home and iron your

shirts, do you?'' She raised her chin in rebellion.

"You've got to be kidding! I'm not going to have to buy all new shirts to replace the ones you would scorch. No, sir. I'll handle the ironing, if you don't mind.''

"Be my guest.''

As the dinner arrived their conversation lulled. They were both hungry enough by now to eat at least three dinners apiece.

"All that loving sure makes you hungry, doesn't it?''

"Shhh!'' Elena frowned. "Someone will hear you.''

"Good.'' He took her hand, folding her fingers in his large grasp. "I want the world to hear me. I love you, Elena Shubert.''

She smiled, praying silently that nothing would ever, ever change the way they felt about one another tonight.

On the way home from the restaurant Elena's head rested on Dave's shoulder as he drove. She had succeeded for several hours to erase the image of Tina Volkowski from her mind, but now in the quiet interior of the car her presence sidled once again into Elena's thoughts. What was she going to do about her? Surely this two-piano concert would not be the deciding factor for which one of the women would claim the title of pianist with the orchestra. Perhaps this was the directors' way of slowly easing her out, giving Tina more parts to play with each performance. As Tina received more attention Elena would slowly fade farther into oblivion.

Elena shifted uneasily against Dave.

"Are you worried about the performance, Elena?"

"Yes," she answered, amazed that his mind was so in tune with hers.

"I listened to you practicing with Tina this afternoon. I know that I'm not exactly what you would call an informed critic, but to my ears you don't have a thing to worry about. Next to her you shine like a supernova."

Elena smiled to herself and snuggled closer to Dave's side. He was her champion. His love would sustain her through this crisis. How wonderful it was to have someone share her fears and worries. How wonderful to have David. How wonderful to be in love!

As much as she tried to force it back, a tainted seed of uncertainty suddenly split open, springing up into Elena's garden of contentment. She had always conceived of herself as a realist, but was she now, with David, dreaming an impossible dream?

Dave glanced contentedly down at Elena's head resting on his shoulder. Their relationship was like a dream come true. He had never believed that it would happen and yet he had continued to hope and believe in miracles. When he noticed the frown that fleetingly creased her brow, he felt a bubble of uneasiness fill his chest.

A chord of fear struck his nerves as he watched her expression. She was worried about her career. She was worried about Tina Volkowski. Would she be able to accept the end when it came?

He had meant it when he said they would still have each other, but she had never made such a comment herself. If she lost her position with the symphony, would she be able to turn to him for support or would she close him out?

He sensed the beginning of a new movement in this glorious symphony that played between them. He clenched his jaw, praying silently that it was not the final movement.

Chapter Ten

"Don't try to tell me how to play the piano, Elena Shubert. I have studied at Julliard since I was seven." Tina's glare and mouth were twisted with derision.

"I'm not trying to tell you how to play the piano, Tina. I am trying to tell you how to play this concerto. You are playing it wrong. And the concert is tomorrow night!"

"I am not playing it wrong!"

"The tempo is much faster through here." Elena took her pencil and put a huge X on Tina's sheet music above the measure she was discussing.

Elena had just about had it. She had tried to be patient, but Tina constantly refused any help or advice. She was belligerent, uncooperative, stubborn, and downright hateful. Elena glanced at her in disgust. And was she going to wear her hair in those ridiculous pigtails on the night of the performance?

"I am going to take a ten-minute break," Elena informed Tina as she grabbed her purse and slipped the strap over her shoulder. "We'll pick it up at *C* when I get back."

Tina glared at Elena's retreating figure moving off the stage. She would get even with her. No one, especially that has-been amateur, was going to tell Tina Volkowski how to play a damn Mozart concerto.

"Excuse me?" Tina was startled out of her murky bog of hate by the low timbre of a man's voice. She glanced up to see that gorgeous hunk of a man to whom Elena erroneously believed she had a claim. "Do you know where Elena is?" Dave asked politely. He knew this was Elena's prime competitor, but he thought it best if he remained neutral in his attitude toward her.

"Hi!" Tina gushed, forcing the infantile frown from her face. "You're Dave Atwell, aren't you?"

"Yes. Do you know where—"

"I just lo-o-ove football players."

Oh, Christ! Dave groaned inwardly, trying to keep a smile on his face. Who did this little nincompoop think she was fooling?

Before he could respond, Tina stood and sidled up to him, tilting her head provocatively in a manner that looked absolutely ridiculous with those two clumps of hair that stuck out at the sides of her ears.

The man really was attractive, Tina decided, getting her first look at him close-up. But even if he had not been good-looking, her hatred for Elena would have spurred her on anyway. Tina thought she could have everything: a position with the symphony that she wasn't good enough to fill and a juicy hunk of a man who obviously needed more of a woman than Elena was. For God's sake, she was thirty years old! Didn't he want someone young and in her prime?

It was obvious, from those other practice sessions when she had seen the two of them together, that they were enamored with each other. But she could change all that. All it took was a little work. And this man made that work look like pure pleasure.

Tina placed her palms flat against Dave's chest and smiled beguilingly up at him.

With infinite patience Dave removed her hands, letting them drop back down to her side. "I have to find Elena, so if you'll excuse me." He turned to walk in the direction Elena had gone.

"Wait!" Tina now realized it was going to take a more direct approach with this one. "I've got a proposition for you."

Dave turned, his eyebrow cocked in dubious amusement. "Oh, really?"

She moved up against him again. "What I have to say should interest you. It concerns your darling Elena."

This time when she placed her hand on his chest, he didn't remove it.

"I know how badly she wants to keep her position with the symphony." Tina gazed up through a thick fringe of false eyelashes. "And, well, I can easily get a spot with a much better orchestra somewhere."

"So why don't you?" Dave's voice was cold and hard, and a swift shiver of apprehension raced down Tina's spine, before it was once again replaced by determination.

"I might . . . if I received a consolation prize." She lifted her other hand to his chest, rubbing her palms across the broad expanse of muscle and bone. "A juicy steak like you for a reward might be just the incentive I need."

"Is that right?" Dave didn't know whether to laugh in her face or knock her flat on the floor. He had never dreamed before that he could hit a woman, but right now the possibility seemed very enticing.

"That's my offer," she added on a businesslike note.

Dave looped his arms around her, pulling her up so tightly against him that her breath was cut off. "Well, let me tell you something, darlin'," he whispered in her ear, causing her to shudder with anticipation. "I'd take you up on your unique proposition, except that—to use your own simpleminded metaphor—spoiled, leftover meat makes me sick to my stomach."

When he let her loose, she stumbled backward several steps. Regaining her balance, she glared at his back as he walked away. "Your precious Elena will pay for this," she hissed, her face flaming from the embarrassment of being rejected by that big oaf.

At that moment Elena was coming back from her break, but Tina had turned back to her piano so quickly Elena noticed nothing amiss.

"Hello!" Her face opened like a soft flower as she looked up at Dave, obviously surprised but delighted to see him waiting for her.

"Hi." He kissed her gently, thankful that she had not been forced to witness Tina's grotesque performance.

"Have you been here long?"

"No." But long enough to see what kind of person you're up against, he wanted to add.

"I had to take a break from Tina for a few minutes," she whispered conspiratorily.

"I can certainly understand why," he said with feeling. "How much longer do you have to practice?"

"About an hour. But then we have rehearsal with the orchestra this afternoon."

"Can you take time out for lunch?" he asked hopefully.

Elena looped her arms around Dave's neck. "Only if you promise to let me eat before we indulge in any after-dinner activities." She batted her eyelashes flirtatiously.

"I'll be back at noon then." Dave laughed a little breathlessly, amazed and at the same time intrigued by this new, frisky Elena.

"Don't be late." She tantalized him with a vampish smile. "Or we might not have time to eat."

Dave expelled a ragged breath as he watched her walk back to her piano, wondering if he would be able to bear the wait until noon.

When he returned promptly at twelve, she was already on the front steps of the concert hall waiting for him. All it took was one look at the hunger in her eyes and he knew they were not going to have time to eat lunch.

"How long did you say you had?" Dave touched her arm, sensing the heat of desire rise in him as he watched her tilt her head provocatively.

"An hour," she answered casually, cocking an eyebrow at him and smiling slyly. "I was under the impression that you football players specialized in fast moves."

"Where?" he asked, breathless with anticipation.

"My house."

"Let's go."

Breaking all existing land speed records, Dave drove his car to Elena's house in two minutes flat.

As they ran from the car, up the stoop, and into the house, they began frantically tearing at each other's clothes, loosening buttons and drawing down zippers with an urgency that kept them breathless. They stood inside the door, their mouths touching and clinging together as they tried to slip from their clothes.

"David, come on," Elena urged, pulling him behind her up the stairs to her loft. At the top of the stairs she turned and their mouths met once again, their tongues joining in the almost desperate exchange of passion.

As they kissed, Elena looped her arms around Dave's neck and pulled him down onto the bed on top of her. He removed his pants while his mouth still clung to hers, then pulled her up into the passionate crescent of his body, immediately urging himself into her and delighting in her responsive words of love.

As their minds and bodies climbed ever higher up the spiral of physical glory, all words were forgotten. They held fast to one another, rising and falling with each successive wave of pleasure that coursed through their bodies, until finally they lay exhausted on the warm, sun-filled beach of fulfillment.

As Elena lay in the curve of Dave's body, basking in the afterglow of physical union, she wondered if they would always feel this intense passion for one another.

"David, how have I ever managed without you!" Elena breathlessly sighed against his damp temple.

Dave covered the expanse of her throat with kisses, before answering. "Neither of us will ever have to manage alone again. We've spent too many years apart."

"I know, and it seems it was so unnecessary. We

could have been together! What were we doing with our lives?''

"Drifting," he answered, dropping gentle kisses on her lips and eyes as he spoke. "No, not drifting. Drowning. And we've both lingered too long in the chambers of the sea."

Pressing her palms upon his cheeks, Elena smiled, but in her eyes was a tinge of sadness. "Tell me, David, please tell me that this love of ours will never drown."

Lowering his lips to hers once more, he convinced her with his hands, and his mouth, and his body. Over and over again.

As the day of the concert dawned, Elena's nerves were frazzled to the nub. Yesterday afternoon, after dropping her off at the music hall, Dave had taken the train to New York for a sports meeting with some of the network brass. So after rehearsal Elena went home, ate a light dinner, and went to bed early. She knew that she was going to need all the sleep she could get before her first performance with Tina.

Now, as she sat up in her bed and watched the early morning sunlight spill like honey across her oak floor, she wondered what the day would bring. Was this light, which trailed in golden rivulets through the window, bringing with it a renewal of her career, or was it instead highlighting the end of the rainbow she had been following all her life?

Butterflies were rampant in her stomach as she dressed in brown corduroy pants and a bulky beige sweater. She rolled up her sleeves and tried to scramble some eggs the way she had seen David make them, but unlike his, they tasted hard and rubbery. Disgusted with herself, she dumped them down the disposal and fixed a piece of toast instead. Then she heated water in the kettle and steeped some very strong Darjeeling tea.

Carrying her cup, she went into the living room and ran through her scales and chords to loosen her fingers. She always felt a little tighter on performance days, but today she could hardly make her fingers work at all!

She played through some easy pieces first, using them as warm-up exercises. Then she opened the Mozart concerto that had been scored for first piano and began methodically winding her way through the melody. She felt that she knew the piece very well, but tonight she must depend on more than her own playing. If Tina screwed up the tempo as she had all week, it would throw the whole piece off. Well, she would at least have this afternoon to work with her one more time. Maybe today Tina would finally get it right.

Elena practiced on the Mozart for an hour, then switched to the pieces she would be playing for another concert this week. She worked on a Beethoven sonata, on Offenbach's "Barcarolle," and on Wagner's *Die Walküre* before stopping at noon for lunch.

While fixing a bite to eat, she wondered how Dave's meetings in New York were going. She could hardly wait to see him tonight after the performance. Just knowing he would be in the audience gave her the courage to meet Tina Volkowski head on.

In the middle of lunch Marilee called to offer much-needed encouragement.

"Break a leg, kid." Marilee sounded totally confident that Elena would play beautifully.

"Can I break Tina's neck instead?" Elena laughed.

"Be my guest. Wish I could be there to see that, but I have this teachers' meeting. Yuk! I hate those things. How's David?"

"Wonderful," Elena sighed.

And Marilee smiled knowingly at the other end of the line.

After a light lunch Elena walked leisurely to the music hall, enjoying the warmth of the afternoon sun. It was so strange how, in all these years, she had never stopped to enjoy the little things in life the way she was now.

Tender buds clustered on still bare branches, promising the inevitable burst of spring. And now that all of the snow was gone, the new thin sprouts of bluegrass were beginning to dot the winter lawns. Despite her preperformance jitters she had to admit that it was truly a glorious day. When she finally arrived at the auditorium, rehearsal was just beginning.

"Cutting it a little close, aren't you, Elena?" Jerard Williams stabbed her with his pointed glare as she rushed in and sat down at the piano. His gaze shifted back and forth between Elena and Tina, who was also seated at her piano, and he sighed, wishing to hell he did not have to put up with this kind of turmoil in his orchestra. Tapping his baton with resignation, he signaled them to begin.

They practiced the Mozart two-piano concerto first and Elena cringed each time Tina botched the tempo. Jerard continually reprimanded her and, at the same time, blamed Elena for not emphasizing to Tina the proper timing.

When they had finished playing, Jerard gave one final warning that the piece had better be perfected by that evening. Then, forgetting the two women, he turned back to the orchestra to practice the next piece, and Tina immediately began gathering up her sheet music to leave.

"Where do you think you are going?" Jerard Williams's booming voice split the air.

"I—I thought I was through," Tina stammered.

"You will leave when rehearsal is over."

"But I'm not playing any other—"

"You will leave when the rest of the musicians leave, Miss Volkowski. Now, you may sit there and twiddle your thumbs if you wish while we practice. But you will sit there, and you will remain silent."

Elena pursed her lips tightly in an effort to hold back the smile that wanted to burst across her face. A red-faced Tina glared with a new dimension of hostility at Elena through the lid of her piano. But Elena had already dropped her gaze back to her keyboard and did not see the dawning of an idea flicker in Tina's eyes, nor did she see the devious smile that curled the girl's lips into a snarl.

By four o'clock rehearsal had ended and the musicians were filing home to eat dinner and dress for tonight's performance.

When she returned home to do the same, Elena stacked some records onto the spindle of the turntable and turned the volume up loud enough to be heard in the upstairs bathroom. Immediately the soothing, languid sounds of "The Swan" from

Saint-Saëns's *Carnival of the Animals* drifted up the stairs, where Elena was peeling off her pants and sweater.

Pulling the large barrette from the back of her hair, she combed her fingers through the crimped waves that twisted over her shoulders and down her back.

Schumann's "Träumerei" played next upon the steam-filled air as Elena ran hot water into the bathtub. Why was she so nervous? she asked herself over and over. She had performed before audiences at least two thousand times in the past eight years. And she had been nervous many times. But this! This performance with Tina was eating at her the way no other had. The beginning or the end. Renewal or destruction. Which was it to be? The beginning of a new phase in her life, when she would be able to have both her music and a loving relationship with David? Or was she to lose her career and thus be forced to depend on him for her moral and financial support?

"Whatever happens, we've got each other." David's words threaded through her mind now, but left little of the reassurance that had been intended when he said this to her. He had been so positive that they could work it out, that nothing was as important as their relationship. She too had been so sure. But now, with this fear of failure clutching at her insides, she couldn't help but wonder. Maybe David was wrong. Perhaps she was being overly idealistic. If she were to lose this job, could she forget the very thing that had carried her through the past twenty-three years of existence and shift all of her devotion to him instead?

No. No. The impact of this revelation stung the backs of her eyes. No. She couldn't give up what she had worked so hard to attain. She wanted David, there was no doubt about that. But she could never be happy if she were dependent upon him. She had to retain her own identity, her own life-style. She wanted both. She had to have both!

Her fists were clenched tightly at her side as she stared into the bathroom mirror. She could not fail tonight! She could not let her life—yes, music was half of her life—and she would not let it end this way.

She shook her arms and hands, trying to loosen the tension that gripped her muscles so tightly. She had to relax. Stepping into the fragrant tub, she tried to force her thoughts into a positive state of mind. She would play beautifully. She could not help but do so. She would play without a flaw and after the performance she and David would dance, and touch, and love one another with the knowledge that each was bringing an important dimension to the relationship. She would be fulfilled in every sense of the word. She closed her eyes, relishing in the absolute certainty that now flowed like a river through her mind. She would have it all!

Elena didn't go to the concert hall until a few minutes before the performance. She didn't want to have to be near Tina any more than was necessary. But despite her effort to avoid her, this wish was not to be granted.

Tina was waiting doggedly for her at the front door, surprising Elena with an expression that was for the first time candid and guileless. Or was this another one of her tricks? Elena wondered. It was definitely the first time she had ever greeted Elena with anything less than scorn.

"Elena? May I talk to you for a minute?" Tina's hands were clasped in front of her and she smiled timidly at Elena.

"I suppose." Elena's eyes narrowed warily, wondering what Tina had up her sleeve.

"Well, y-you see," Tina began, stammering, "I think I need to be honest with you about some things. There are some things that need to be set straight. I'm sure Dave told you—"

"David? Told me?" What on earth did David have to do with all of this?

"You mean he didn't tell you?" Tina feigned a look of surprise.

Elena's jaw tightened with the chill that rippled through her. "Maybe you'd better tell me," she said gently, berating herself for standing here talking to Tina. She did not need this kind of distraction right before an important concert.

"I tried to take Dave Atwell away from you." Tina's admission dropped like a blunt object from her mouth.

"What!" *Don't tell me these things before a performance! Don't tell me!*

"You have so much, Elena, and...well, I was jealous. Now I know how silly I was being," she hurried on. "I mean, you and Dave are obviously in love and even though it was difficult for me to accept, especially when he put his arms around me, I knew—"

"Put his arms around you!" Elena tried to will the

angry flush away from her face. David put his arms around Tina Volkowski!

"Oh, I forgot." Tina smiled artlessly. "He didn't tell you. Well, really, Elena, it was nothing. I mean he definitely cares more for you than for me, so I decided that I wasn't going to keep trying to defeat you in that way."

"Why are you telling me all of this, Tina?" Elena didn't like the sound of that last phrase at all. Defeat you in that way.

"Because I wanted you to know where I stand."

"And where is that?" Elena's nerves were so wound up inside her stomach they were like corkscrews. And on top of that, she was becoming more and more distrustful of Tina's motives for this little tête-à-tête.

"I've thought quite a bit about that." Tina's chin jutted out and her face began to glow with her customary arrogance. "I've decided that I'm too talented to waste my time on a relationship with a man. Men are wonderful, of course. But I have never had to go hunting for one to satisfy my needs." She patted her hair lightly, but hurried on when she noticed that Elena was losing interest. "My point is that, with talent such as mine, I should devote all of my time to music. Therefore, I've decided to let you have your Dave Atwell."

"That's very gracious of you, Tina. Now if you'll excuse me, I have a performance." Elena swerved around Tina and started walking down the hallway.

"Wait a minute, Elena. I'm not finished."

"Yes, you are."

"No, that's where you're wrong. You see," she continued when she once again had Elena's attention, "I'm letting you have your man because that is all you will have left. I feel a bit sorry for you and I don't want you to end up with nothing. You're going to need someone to lean on."

"Don't make me laugh, Tina," Elena retorted, though she had no intention of laughing. She was tied up in so many knots by now, she was beginning to worry if she could relax enough to play.

"I don't intend to make you laugh, Elena. I intend to crush you."

Elena's eyes widened in a sudden flash of fear when she heard the deadly tone that emanated from Tina's mouth.

"After tonight you will never play with this symphony or any other symphony again. I am going to destroy you!"

With that final warning Tina smiled sweetly and stalked off, leaving Elena more shaken than she had ever been in her life.

She wrapped her arms around her stomach when she shuddered, wondering what was going to happen to her on this fateful night. She knew it was ridiculous to let Tina psych her out like this, but she couldn't help it. She had never known a threat such as this. She had never known a person who was so determined to win that she would walk over everyone in her path.

But, then, look at it realistically, she told herself. *Tina hasn't gotten the piece right once this week. Why should you worry that tonight will be any different? She will blend in with the orchestra at best,*

*and you will hold center stage. She's trying to upset
you with mental torment so that you will play badly.
But you are stronger than that. You've been playing
under pressure for too many years for this to get to
you. Loosen up, dammit!*

Despite her courageous-sounding lecture to herself, an apprehensive shiver raced down her spine as
she thought of Tina's threat. And too a flash of
David's arms around Tina's body wedged like a sliver
of sharp glass in her throat. Why didn't David tell
her? She cringed to think what his responses had
been to Tina's attempt to entice him.

Swallowing hard to hold back her fear and suspi-
cions, Elena walked slowly down the hall toward the
low, rumbling sounds of voices.

Greeting and visiting with some of the musician
friends she had worked with for eight years, she grad-
ually began to work off some of her nervous jitters.
Tina was nowhere to be seen and that fact alone was
enough to ease a substantial portion of the tension in
her mind.

Elena watched as the musicians wound through the
rows of folding chairs, seated themselves, and began
running through various measures of the pieces, tuning and listening for the precise tones from their instruments. The scene was a reassuring one, one she
had watched and taken part in for so many years.
This was her life. She couldn't let that ruthlessly ambitious intruder take it from her!

Elena turned when she felt a gentle hand on her
back. She smiled into the eyes of a middle-aged woman she had known for years. The editor of *Virtuoso
Magazine* smiled back.

"Elena, my dear." She shook her grayed head sadly. "I was sickened by the news I heard this afternoon. We are going to miss you so much."

Elena stared at the older woman, bewildered by the statement. Was the woman leaving the magazine? Perhaps she was going to work for another magazine.

"I just can hardly believe that this will be your last performance!" she lamented.

Last...performance! What was she talking about? Where did she hear such a thing?

"When we got the news this afternoon, all of us on the staff were so shocked. At first we didn't know whether to believe it, but—"

Oh, my God! Her last performance! They had decided to replace her with Tina. But why hadn't she been informed? How could they have announced it to the press without even informing her first? She turned away from the editor, tears glistening on her lashes.

What was she going to do? She had to get away from here. She couldn't possibly play tonight. Not with everyone knowing that this was her last performance. Even the members of the orchestra must know by now. And no one had said a word to her! How could they have done this to her?

Her head jerked back and forth frantically, her gaze sweeping the stage wings in panic. She had to find Jerard. She had to tell him that she couldn't play. She wasn't in the right frame of mind. Knowing what she now knew, she would never be able to perform. Her hands were wringing fitfully at her side as she continued to search for the conductor.

"Elena? Is everything all right?" The editor's concern tore through the shroud of strangling anguish that had wrapped itself around Elena, shutting off all air, all hope. "Are you all right?"

"Yes," she managed to answer the editor, who scurried away in embarrassment as soon as Elena assured her that she was fine. She had never meant to say something to upset the performer. She only wanted to let her know how she would be missed.

"Let's go, Elena." Jerard walked into view and signaled to her, totally oblivious of the agony that was written all over her face. Only one person was aware of it. Elena's stupefied gaze traveled from Jerard's calm expression to Tina standing next to him. On her face was the most hideous smile of satisfaction Elena had ever seen.

Her gaze sprinted back and forth between Jerard, who was conferring with a stagehand about sound equipment, and Tina, whose eyes blazed with her triumph, as the realization slowly dawned on her. It was over. Her career was over. Tina Volkowski had won. And no one, except Tina, had had the courage to tell her. In the hallway a few minutes earlier Tina had said this would be her last performance. At the time Elena had wanted to laugh. Now she wanted nothing more than to scream.

But as the victorious smile hovered on Tina's face, Elena drew on a strength she didn't know she had. She would not cry in front of them. She would go on stage and she would play. She would not give them the satisfaction of watching her crumble.

As the maestro and the two pianists walked onto the stage, Elena heard none of the hand-clapping approval that accompanied them. In her mind the applause was metamorphosed into the words of the editor. *"I can hardly believe that this will be your last performance.... Last performance.... Last performance...."* Everyone in the audience knew. Everyone in the orchestra knew. The stagehands knew. The press knew. David, sitting in the center aisle seat that Elena had procured for him, knew.

Sitting down on her hard piano bench, in front of the Steinway keyboard she had insisted on using for so many years, claiming that it brought her luck, Elena felt all eyes riveted on her. They were staring, peering into her soul, prying into her feelings, spearing her with their judgmental eyes.

From his position in the audience Dave had a perfect view of Elena. Dressed in her long black dress, her chestnut hair pulled back from her face and falling down her back in thick scalloped waves, she elicited from him that same tugging reaction of desire. In this moment he wanted to be that man of her childhood fantasy, the one who rose from the audience and lifted her from the piano. He wanted to hear her music, but he wanted her in his arms while he listened. He felt a pride in her accomplishments and, at the same time, he felt an antagonism for that shiny black piano that demanded so much of her time and energy. He longed for her to want him as badly as he wanted her.

Elena couldn't concentrate on anything but the pain of everyone knowing that this was her last night at this piano. Though her fingers lifted to strike the first key on cue, her mind was not with the music. It was with those eyes from the audience, the orchestra, the conductor, and the other pianist as they all watched her final performance.

She tried to count the beats in order to focus her concentration on the music, and it was with sickening astonishment that she realized Tina was playing her part flawlessly. There was no mistake in timing. There was no improvisation. She was playing the piece as if she had played it all her life. Elena now realized she had been duped. All week Tina had been playing against her, pretending she couldn't get it right. She had known how it was supposed to be all along. She had played Elena for a monumental fool!

Elena counted the beats, trying to hold back her tears of defeat. One and a, two...and three and a, four...and...Elena stared incredulously at her fingers hovering and shaking above the keyboard. The notes! She was supposed to be playing the notes. Her memory had failed her! Where were the notes? She was aware of the slight hesitation from the orchestra before they recovered sufficiently to continue playing. Jerard turned around to glance sharply at Elena.

Oh, God, why couldn't she remember? She continued to stare at her hands frozen uselessly above the keys. Then, in one shattering, apocalyptic moment, the melody once again began to fill the air. Elena sat still, listening to the sounds and wondering why her fingers were not moving. And then, with a nauseous surge, she realized the music was not coming from her own piano. It was coming from Tina's. Tina had memorized not only her own part, but Elena's as well. She had somehow known that this moment would come, and she had been ready for it.

Dave's sweating hands were gripping the arms of his chair, his eyes glued on Elena's small figure. What was wrong with her? Something was happening. Had she forgotten the piece? His fingers dug deeper into the upholstery and every fiber in his being was trained on making her remember. *Remember the notes, Elena. Dammit, remember!* He felt a pain in his gut when Tina began playing Elena's part. Every muscle in his body turned flaccid, defeat etched into the core of his body as surely as it had into Elena's.

Elena tasted the sour flavor of defeat in her mouth. She listened to the notes Tina was playing and finally, with resigned dedication, picked them up herself. As effortlessly as she had played Elena's part, Tina went back to her own accompaniment.

Although the memory lapse had lasted less than a minute, Elena knew that everyone in the audience was aware of her mistake. Her last concerto, and she had shamefully mangled it.

As the piece came to an uneventful close, Elena knew that the plaudits from the audience were not for her; they were for Tina's brilliant performance. The crowd had accepted her as their own pianist, and they were welcoming her with their thunderous applause.

Chapter Eleven

The lights for intermission flooded the auditorium, drawing away the spotlight from Elena's distraught profile.

Dave knew he had to go backstage, for he was sure that Elena would need him now. And he didn't want her to have to go through this alone. Threading his way against the flow of traffic, he moved through the crowd and headed up the side stairs to the wings.

Elena remained seated for several minutes while the rest of the musicians stood and stretched their muscles. Finally she too stood and walked to the wings where she had to face the stone-cold stare of Jerard Williams.

He glared at her, dragging her to him with his frozen features. As she stood in front of him, she looked him squarely in the eye, trying desperately to squelch the trembling in her limbs.

"So." His voice boomed above all others on the wings, drawing unwanted attention to their conversation. "All of this time I've been worried about how Miss Volkowski would perform this evening, and it was you I should have worried about."

"Why didn't you tell me this was my last performance?" Elena's eyes were brimming with the tears she had kept back for over an hour, and her voice croaked with accusation.

"Believe me," Jerard bellowed, and Elena was sure that the symphony patrons in the lobby could hear, "if I had known that you were going to disembowel the entire Mozart concerto, I would most definitely have told you this was your last performance."

"Are you trying to pretend you didn't know ahead of time that I was to be fired?"

"What in the hell are you talking about?"

"I'm talking about the directors' decision to replace me with Tina Volkowski."

"There has been no decision."

"But...the editor of *Virtuoso Magazine*? She told me...just before we began tonight...she said... you mean, this was not to be my last performance with the orchestra?" Elena's voice was choked with disbelief.

"That is the most preposterous thing I have ever heard!" Jerard's face was indignant. "Do you think you would not be informed of such a decision?"

"I don't know! I don't know!" Elena was shaking her head back and forth, crying and mumbling to herself at the same time. "That's why I had the memory lapse, Jerard. I couldn't think straight because I was told that it was my last performance and I thought I was the only one who didn't know. Who could have started such a vicious—" Elena raised her head sharply, staring across the wings at the one person who could have perpetrated such a cruel lie.

Tina was leaning against a wall, placidly checking her fingernail polish for flaws. She glanced up at Elena, then looked back down at her nails.

Tina! She told the editor that it was to be Elena's

last performance. There was not one ounce of truth to the rumor at all!

"The only person who has most likely made this your last performance is you, Elena Shubert." This time Jerard's comment was issued as a low growl. His hand was on her arm and his face was menacingly close to hers, a snarl playing ferociously upon his lips. "If I did not know how well you can play, I would recommend to the board that you be fired on the spot."

When Dave pushed through the crowd and first saw Elena, it was as she cowered beneath the glowering hulk of Jerard Williams. That bastard had his hands on her! All Dave could think about was Williams touching her, his unforgivable behavior toward her at his apartment, trying to force her to make love to him so that she could keep her job. "I ought to kill him," Dave growled savagely to himself, circling in slowly for the kill.

Elena was fully aware of Jerard's anger, yet she also sensed in his eyes and his words a glimmer of hope. He did not say that he was going to recommend that she be fired. He even admitted that she played well. There was still hope!

As suddenly as the glimpse of assurance entered her mind, she watched it snuffed out before her very eyes. Jerard was wrenched from her and thrust forcefully against the wall. As her focus sharpened she saw with frightening clarity that Dave had pinned her conductor to the wall.

"David! My God, what are you doing?" She was conscious of the crowd that had gathered, and she was also aware, very aware, of the livid color in Jerard Williams's face.

What was David saying to him? Elena tried to concentrate on the words. "Ever touch...again... break every bone...shove that baton up—"

By the time several men had pulled Dave away from the conductor, Elena was in a state of panic. Why was David doing this to her? What possessed him to attack her conductor?

Jerard spun around to her, glaring with the most indignant wrath she had ever seen. "You!" He pointed an accusing finger at Elena. "I've had it with you. Get out of my sight and out of my orchestra!" He quickly turned and looked for Tina, who was hovering confidently on the fringe of the crowd.

"What can you play?" he brusquely asked her.

"I can play the Rimski-Korsakov that Elena was going to play," she answered excitedly.

"Can you play it well?" he demanded.

"Perfectly." Her head tilted upward in a superior angle, and her eyes shone with a self-absorption equaled only by the conductor's own egoism.

"Good." He nodded, satisfied. "You will play."

As the musicians filed back on stage Tina passed within a breath of Elena. "Good-bye, Elena," she laughed disdainfully, before flicking a cursory glance at Dave. "Tarzan over there will take care of you."

As she walked onto the stage Elena had the most violent urge to stick out her foot and trip Tina. But instead, she watched lethargically as the moon-faced doll walked into the arena that had been Elena's life.

"It's okay, honey." Dave placed a reassuring hand on her arm and was surprised when she pivoted sharply and glared hatefully at him.

"Okay? Okay?" she whispered venomously. "You have just made sure that nothing. . . nothing is okay." She stalked away from him, grabbing her coat and heading out the back door into the alley.

Dave hung back, stupefied by her anger. What was she mad at him for? And what did she mean, he had made sure that nothing was okay? Quickly catching up with her, he grasped her elbow, turning her to face him.

As soon as his fingers touched her coat, she yanked her arm free as if she had been burned.

"What in the hell is the matter with you?" he asked, stunned by her behavior.

"Me? What do you think you were doing in there?" she virtually screamed at him. "You just lost me my job!"

Dave jumped as if he had been electrocuted. "What—what do you mean? Williams was threatening you!"

"He was acting like any normal conductor would do. He was furious with me for blowing the concerto."

"He had his hands on you," Dave offered as an excuse.

"So what?"

"So what? The man practically raped you the other night. Or—" Dave pulled back slightly, narrowing his eyes on Elena "—maybe that was a lie. Maybe you went to his place to try to secure your position. Perhaps it was you, and not him, who tried to use sex as a form of contract. I mean, after all, you did try it with me."

Elena swung back her arm and brought it forward to slap Dave. But before it reached his face, he grasped her wrist in an iron grip.

"Is that it, Elena?" he demanded. "He rejected you?"

She glared at him as her entire body shook, reflecting an anger too profound to even allow her to respond.

Knowing beyond a shadow of a doubt that she would never do such a thing as he had intimated, Dave was too upset to curb his tongue. He had thought he was helping her. And now she was acting as if he alone had brought about the end of her career.

"How low will you stoop to keep all of this, Elena? Does this job, with this symphony, mean that much to you?"

"Nothing else means anything!" Elena cried, knowing in the back of her mind that tomorrow she would regret those words. She watched as Dave's face fell into a mask of carefully concealed anguish. Why was she saying this to him? Why couldn't she let him love her and take care of her? Why was she so afraid to lean on someone else?

When Dave spoke, his voice was solemn and low, but it took every ounce of strength in his body not to violently shake some sense into her head. "What about the times we've made love? Does that not mean anything?"

Elena quickly shifted her gaze from him, her emotions too jumbled to allow her to think straight. All she knew was that she had lost the most important career opportunity she had ever had. There was no doubt about it this time. She had lost. And because of David's offensive behavior, Jerard would never forgive her. It was a young world, he had told her. Young and fiercely competitive. Maybe she didn't fit in anymore. Perhaps she was past her prime.

But did that mean she was supposed to give up the dream she had carried for so many years and shift all of her love and energy and dependence to a man instead? If she were going to be with David, surely she should bring something to the relationship other than her dependence.

"I guess I just received my answer," Dave said, watching her silent profile. "You really played me for a fool, Elena." He laughed bitterly. "I really thought what we had was—"

Elena held her breath as Dave paused, afraid to hear the words he was going to use. She didn't want to hear that their relationship was special. That they loved each other. That they were meant as a timeless duet. She waited, her muscles clenched tightly until she heard his low curse.

"Well, it's been fun," he added, his voice laden with sarcasm. "We'll have to do it again sometime." He turned and stalked away, leaving her standing in the alley, her tears finally free to fall as she covered her face, sobbing into her bare hands.

Behind her, through the back door of the stage, she could hear the strains of Rimski-Korsakov's "Song of India" rising from the piano.

She had been walking for two hours, pacing ever onward, going nowhere. Now she was once again standing in front of the magnificent old music hall.

The lights were still on, though the musicians and the spectators had all gone home.

Elena pulled her coat more tightly around her, shivering as much from the awesome beauty of the structure as from the cold.

Ground lighting illuminated the shrubbery at the base of the building and shot cylinders of light up the marble facade and the front colonnade. She shook her head in bewilderment as she thought of how many times had she walked up these palatial steps without noticing the grandeur of the building, without paying any heed at all to how well tended the gardens were and how well preserved the sixty-five-year-old structure was.

She glanced at the roman numerals that graced the portico. Built in 1918, it had withstood decades of economical depression and social criticism. She remembered the campaign that was waged a few years ago to raze the run-down auditorium. A few staunch revivalists engaged in a successful counterattack and the building was rejuvenated to its former glory.

Wearily Elena climbed the steps and opened one set of double doors. Walking into the foyer, she could smell the antiseptic aroma of clean wax the janitors had spread across the marble floor. Stepping gingerly so as not to destroy the shine, Elena opened another set of double doors that led into the auditorium.

Standing in the aisle, she looked all around her at the empty, dimly-lit arena. The Greek statues that punctuated the interior walls were poised and alert, as if wary about this intruder who had entered their euphonious sanctum.

Elena removed her coat and sat down in an aisle seat, leaning back and staring at the almost magical elegance of the gold and crystal chandeliers that hung from the ceiling. They had now been dimmed with a raostat to a yellow glow, leaving only the stage in full light.

The orchestra chairs and podium were still assembled, the Baldwin that Tina preferred occupying left center stage. The Steinway that Elena always used had obviously been rolled away after the two-piano number.

Elena ran her hands along the upholstered armrests of the chair and closed her eyes. Sweeping down the canyons of her mind, she could hear the instruments tuning up, then slowly the discordant sounds died and in their place arose the rich, dynamic tones of Edvard Grieg's Concerto in A Minor, the first concerto Elena had ever played with this symphony. The music ebbed and flowed, alternating between allegro and adagio, as she leaned back in her seat and listened with rapturous wonder.

After a while she opened her eyes and stared at the empty stage, the still piano, and recognized the sounds as only those of her own mind. Wiping a few stray tears from her cheeks, she stood and, straightening her shoulders and elevating her chin, left the auditoriuim for the last time, without looking back.

Dave paced his hotel room as he had every night that week, running his fingers through his hair in agitation. He picked up a stack of papers from the couch and carried them to the small table set in one corner of the room. Sitting down, he tried to begin memorizing the names, the dates, and the statistics on the players for the next game.

Damn! He threw the papers into a heap on the floor, and stood up to begin pacing once again. He had never been so furious in his life. Nor had he ever felt this hopeless frustration. He had really believed that Elena loved him. He thought that she felt as strongly about their relationship as he did.

Well, he was sick of it! She had led him around by the nose for too long. All the years she had eaten into his subconscious, making it impossible for him to find someone else to replace her image. And these past few weeks, drawing him even closer, to the point where he didn't think he could make it without her. *Damn her! And damn yourself, Dave Atwell, for being such a stupid fool!*

He grabbed his key and left the room, slamming the door behind him. Downstairs in the bar, he tried to drown Elena with glass after glass of bourbon. He would drink her into oblivion. He would push her back into that chamber of the sea where she belonged, where she obviously wanted to remain. He should never have tried to make her face what she was totally incapable of facing. She was not meant to be a part of the real world.

He was staring broodingly into the half-empty glass of bourbon when someone tapped his shoulder.

"Time to close it up, mister," the bartender informed him. "Hey, don't I know you? Yeah, aren't you that—that football player for...let's see.... Oh, I can't remember which team. Are you him?"

Dave looked up at the blurred image of the man.

Football player. Announcer. Fool. What in the hell was he?

He slowly shook his head at the bartender, who was now grinning from ear to ear, positive that Dave was that football player. "No," Dave answered. "I'm not him."

The smile on the bartender's face faded and was replaced by a look of disgust over having to remove one more drunk patron from the bar. "Well, let's go, buddy. Time to call it a night."

Dave lifted himself wearily from the barstool, weaving his way through the empty tables, through the door, and somehow managing to make his way in the elevator and up to his room.

Once inside he dropped his key on the table and, rummaging through the desk drawer, found his address book. He weaved unsteadily as he flipped through the pages, until he finally located the number he wanted.

Sitting on the edge of the bed, he dialed, but had to redial several times before he did it correctly. When the silky, purring voice answered the phone, Dave immediately felt his blood turning to fire. *I'm going to erase you from my mind, Elena Shubert. Whatever it takes, I'm going to purge your image from my life.*

"Kristin? This is Dave Atwell."

"Dave," she sighed sleepily, and he had the sudden vision of the woman lying naked between satin sheets. "I was wondering if I was ever going to hear from you again."

His voice was slightly slurred, but he managed to

get the words out, knowing he had to do this if he was ever going to forget Elena. "I was wondering if the ski trip was still on for Vail."

"Yes!" Though sleepy, she sounded excited, causing Dave's pulse to bound with anticipation. "There will always be a place for you, Dave. In fact, it might be a good idea to get together ahead of time to discuss our...plans for the trip. Say tomorrow night?"

Elena's impassioned cry that "Nothing else means anything" hurled through his mind for the hundredth time, and he knew with absolute certainty that she had meant every word she uttered.

"Tomorrow night. I'll be there, Kristin."

Chapter Twelve

It had been the longest week of Elena's life. Never had time forged by with such leaden steps. She had moved restlessly through the days, passing from one insignificant task to another.

First she would sit at the piano, her fingers wandering aimlessly over the keys. Familiar melodies wove through the air as she played the pieces she had performed for so many years.

Then she tried to learn how to operate her washer and dryer, but gave up after soap billowed from underneath the lid onto her floor.

She checked and rechecked her financial situation, wondering how long she could manage without a job. She spent hours on the phone with Marilee, bracing herself for the very real possibility that she would end up teaching piano to gradeschoolers also.

She stopped watching for the signs of spring, knowing that fair weather would not come into her life this year to melt away the winter chill within her. Even hell, it seemed, had its own vast polar regions where nothing but pain was allowed to multiply and grow.

As the pain increased, so too did the sense of inadequacy and doubts. Why had she not foreseen this moment? She wasn't stupid, and yet she had wrapped her entire life into one neat little package, never anticipating for a moment that it would eventually come unglued at the seams. Maybe stupid wasn't the right epithet to heap upon herself. Maybe blind was more accurate. Pathetic emotional blindness. A perfect label for a psychological syndrome. Clinics could be set up, theses written, studies undertaken of every pianist, or every artist, or any others who were bent exclusively on self-fulfillment.

What kind of curse had her parents inflicted on her? She rubbed her temples as she contemplated the thought that had entered her head. No, she knew she really could not blame them. She had been blessed and her parents—her father had merely tried to help her realize the full potential of her talent. And she had never shown them that she wanted anything else. She had never complained about the long hours of practice. She had never rebelled against the isolation that was forced upon her.

She had loved her father, and her music had given him so much pleasure, so much pride. But what about her own pleasure? It was absurd to even ask herself such a question. Of course she loved her music. Her pleasure in it had sprung from her devotion to it, her satisfaction in a job well done, her need to find a central core around which to base her life.

It was on a morning when Elena was feeling particularly awash in self-pity that a sliver of warm light pierced the frozen, arctic wasteland of her soul.

Elena stood gazing out the back window of her apartment, a frown creasing her brow and darkening the gray of her eyes. An idea had settled upon her suddenly and she wasn't sure she liked it at all. She wasn't sure she wanted to know the truth. She mulled it around a bit, trying to envision the flow of the conversation. *Hello, Mother? Tell me honestly now, you've always hated my devotion to the piano, haven't you?*

She sighed heavily and turned toward the phone. Whatever her mother's response, Elena knew she needed some guidance. She had never listened to her mother enough in the past. But maybe it was time to listen to someone other than herself. With hesitant fingers she dialed the California number.

Dave climbed the steps to the front door of Kristin's apartment. As she opened the door, he had the most peculiar feeling that he should tilt his head sideways to look at her. Her black hair was pulled on top of her head, tied in a bun that sat purposefully lopsided. It gave her entire face a catawampus appearance. Forcefully restraining himself from frowning, Dave concentrated on the rest of her appearance. With it he could find no fault.

Kristin was dressed in a tight red jersey dress that revealed and authenticated every one of her most abundant curves. Her lips and fingernails were painted the exact color of her dress.

"It's been a long time, Dave," she mewed like a sultry cat.

"Too long," he agreed as he watched the sway of her hips when she slinked seductively to the coat closet. She slipped into a black mink, and Dave couldn't help but wonder what she had to do to get that coat. Her salary as a sales clerk would hardly provide for such luxuries.

"Where are we going tonight?" She flipped the

lock on her door and stepped out into the night air with Dave.

"Anywhere but the symphony," he mumbled, but not too softly for Kristin not to hear.

She glanced sideways at him and frowned. She had heard through the grapevine that he was hung up on some musician. But she assumed since he called her for a date, the relationship must be over. Was he on the rebound? Was she to be a vehicle for his sexual frustrations? Kristin smiled to herself, hoping that the evening would progress at least that far.

"I never have gone in for that long-haired music anyway," she said, unaware of the withering look he sent her way. "But there is an Italian place that I have been dying to try."

Oh, no! Dave cringed. Please don't let it be the one where he took Elena.

"It's called Armando's and I understand it's ver-r-ry romantic."

Dave flinched imperceptibly, thinking of how special it had been when he took Elena there. Damn! Well, he did ask Kristin out. And he couldn't very well expect to feed her at McDonald's. With a sense of impending doom Dave drove the two of them to Armando's, she with romance on her mind and he trying not to think of romance or of the woman that word invoked.

Once seated in the restaurant, Dave ignored the surroundings. *Don't think about the past. Focus on this woman across from you, idiot. She is the only one who matters now.*

"The lasagna is very good here," he suggested.

"No, I think I'll have the linguini. I understand the clam sauce is wonderful."

From that moment on Dave knew that the evening was doomed to failure. Everything they said, every place they went, brought with it reminders of Elena. He continuously compared this hardened black-haired vixen with his soft, gray-eyed, chestnut-haired Elena.

His Elena! What a joke! He was going to have to stop thinking of her that way. But would he ever be able to admit that they did not belong to one another? She had been snuggled among the folds of his thoughts for twelve years. And now that he had actually made love to her—held her all through the night—how could he possibly forget her?

Later that evening Dave and Kristin met Jerry Monroe and his date at the nightclub in Dave's hotel. As Dave danced with Kristin he felt her rubbing up against him, letting him know that she was available for the night if he wanted her. The music and the drinks and the constant thrust of Kristin's hips against his own began to lift Elena's image away from the forefront of his mind. But still she hovered nearby, never quite disappearing altogether, yet not forcing her presence onto the scene.

Dave pulled Kristin's body more tightly against him as they danced. If he could forget—just for tonight.

He lowered his mouth to her neck, and he automatically compared the overpowering smell of her musk perfume with the sweet honeysuckle scent of Elena.

After several more rounds of drinks Dave was in a fog and was, therefore, agreeable to any idea the group suggested. Jerry's was that they all go back to Dave's room for more partying. Not particularly caring where they went, Dave drained the last of the bourbon from his glass and tossed a substantial tip onto the barmaid's tray. He took Kristin's hand in his, no longer seeing anything more than a body to ease his physical and mental aches.

They all four stopped in the hotel liquor store and bought a couple of bottles of wine, then rode the glass elevator up to the tenth floor, leading Dave to his own room.

Elena paced off every square inch of her house. There was not a corner that had not been touched, stared at, stepped on, or damned. Tonight was the same as every night had been since the performance. She had taken a bath and donned her long nightgown out of habit, but she knew with certainty that she would be unable to sleep. She went to the kitchen for a glass of water. She flipped on a stack of records. She turned off the record player. She played a few notes on the piano. She cursed the piano. She climbed her stairs and lay across the bed. She closed her eyes, only to have them immediately fly open again. She pushed herself from the bed. She paced.

Her mother's words threaded through her mind, forcing her to remember them and think about them. *"Nothing will fill your days like love, Elena. No music in the world can compensate for the lack of love."*

Elena squeezed her eyes shut tightly, remembering

the entire conversation. It had been a painful dialogue, but one that in the end cleansed the wounds that both women had harbored for so many years. For the first time Elena saw her mother as another woman, one who had dreams of her own, plans for her own life, hopes for her daughter's life. Hopes and dreams that were dashed. Elena realized now that she—and her father to a certain extent—had shut her mother out of her life. Because her mother didn't approve of Elena's obsession with music, Elena had tuned her out, using her as one might use a domestic servant.

Yes, the conversation had been a good thing. It would take a long time for the wounds to completely heal between them, but at least they had taken the first curative step.

Her thoughts sifted back through the debris to her mother's words about love. Nothing, she had said, could fill one's days like love. It had sounded so simple when her mother had said it. Call David, she had advised. Let him know how sorry you are. Why did that now seem like such a monumental step to take?

But she was right, Elena admitted. She did have to call him! She had to try and apologize for what she had said to him. She hadn't meant it. She loved David. She knew that now. He had only tried to protect her and care for her, and she had repaid him by telling him that he meant nothing to her. If only he knew that he was the only thing that meant anything to her! All these years she had let her life revolve around what she had always thought of as a blessing. She had been engulfed by it and had never known what living was all about.

But when something became so powerful in a person's life that it even destroyed love, it could no longer be considered a blessing. It was an affliction.

She knew she must at least try to explain this to David. She had to let him know that she had been wrong, that his love meant everything to her. Elena picked up the phone and dialed the number of his hotel, and when the operator answered, she gave her the number.

"Room Ten twenty-one, please."

"Do you have any ice, darling?" Kristin purred, though her voice was now thick and slurred.

"I'll get some." Dave grabbed the ice bucket, grateful for any task that would take him away from the woman who was lounging so possessively upon his bed. The same bed where he and Elena had made love only a few nights ago. As he stepped into the hall and turned to close the door, he watched Kristin's high-heeled shoe drop to the floor beside the bed. Sighing, he wondered again what he was doing with this woman. God, as much as he had drunk, he probably wouldn't even be able to find the bed, much less perform to her satisfaction!

Weaving down the hallway, Dave heard, somewhere in the fog of his mind, the sound of telephones ringing. The blood in his head was pounding so hard he was sure that every phone in the hotel was clamoring at the same time. Must be an emergency, he decided with unconcern, still heading in staggering but relentless and undaunted pursuit of the ice machine.

Elena gripped the receiver so tightly her knuckles turned white when the telephone in Dave's room was answered. The voice that said hello at the other end of the line was soft and sultry, yet it seemed to Elena as if the feminine sound were screaming a high-pitched wail over and over in her ears. She slammed the receiver back onto its cradle.

A woman in David's room! Could the operator have connected her with the wrong room? She picked up the phone again and dialed, once more asking for David Atwell's room.

"Hello?" The same sultry voice purred across the wires.

"I—I'm sorry," Elena stammered. "I must have the wrong room." She quickly hung up the phone, her cheeks glowing bright red from the call. She felt as if she had trespassed, had peered into someone's window and seen something illicit and tasteless.

She now knew that the other night at the music hall she had effectively destroyed the strains of music between herself and David as surely as she had mutilated the concerto on stage.

She ran to the bathroom and washed her hands with soap and water over and over again, trying to wash away the slimy feel of the telephone and the damage she had done to David. As she scrubbed her flesh the words of Shakespeare entered uninvited into her mind, lambasting her with the truth of what her life had been.

> Life's but a walking shadow, a poor player
> That struts and frets his hour upon the stage,
> And then is heard no more; it is a tale
> Told by an idiot, full of sound and fury,
> Signifying nothing.

After five full minutes Elena realized that, no matter how much she tried to wash away her blame, her hands would not come clean—not even with "all the perfumes of Arabia."

In a stupor of defeat and self-pity she walked slowly to the piano, her solace in times of loneliness and pain. She sat down and began absently toying with a finger exercise.

Out of the corner of her eye she glimpsed the corner of a piece of staff paper tucked midway in a two-foot stack of sheet music.

Bending down to reach it, she pulled the paper up and stared at the composition she had played that day for David. How long ago that seemed! She remembered his enthusiasm over the piece, and she inadvertently smiled. You could be another Burt Bacharach, he had exclaimed. Or a Marvin Hamlisch!

She slowly began playing the melody with one hand, eventually adding the chords with her left. As she played, the music began to grow and expand, chipping through the frozen ice cap that had surrounded her for so many days.

The composition was almost finished. Elena had spent the past week working almost exclusively on it. She had to admit that it was, in fact, the only thing that had kept her going these past few days. And she also had to confess that David had been right. The piece she wrote was good! She had always thought of it as a hobby before, but now she saw it as a valid possibility for her future. Someday, who knows, she might even be able to sell one of her songs.

She already knew what she would do with this piece once it was finished. She would add the lyrics she already had in mind for it, and then she would send it to David. She realized it was too late to let him know what a fool she had been, but at least she could offer the music as an apology, inadequate as it might be. By finishing this one thing she would let him know that she had listened to him, that his opinion had mattered to her. Maybe too the words would express what she felt—what she had always felt—about him. Someday perhaps she would have the courage to tell him all of this face to face. But for now her music would have to do it for her.

The telephone rang twice before she paid attention and stopped making notations on the staff paper with her pencil.

"Hello?" she answered absently, her mind still playing with different possibilities for the melody.

"Elena, my sweet! Hello? Hello?" the man repeated when she didn't respond.

"Alexi?" Elena's mind finally synthesized the voice at the other end of the line. "Is that you, Alexi?"

"Who else, my dove?"

"Where are you?"

"I'm in Saint Louis. I am now the permanent conductor of this orchestra. I assumed you would have heard," he added on a bruised note.

"Of course I heard, and I'm so happy for you."

"And I heard about you too. But not to worry," he hurried ahead. "I have a wonderful opportunity for you here."

Elena tried to concentrate, but her thoughts were

still trained on finding that elusive measure that would tie her piece together. "Just a minute, Alexi." Forgetting that he was calling long distance, she set down the telephone and began drawing notes on the paper, the sound of each one playing in her head. She erased one that wasn't right and replaced it with another.

"Elena! Elena!" The low shout from the phone finally pierced her concentration.

"Hello?"

"Elena! What in heaven's name are you doing?"

"Oh, Alexi, I'm sorry. I was. . .I had something I had to take care of. Now, what were you saying?"

"I was saying that there is an opportunity for you here with the symphony."

"Oh?" she asked with disinterest. "What is that?"

"Well, before I tell you, I hope you will show a little more enthusiasm. You want to work for another orchestra, don't you?"

"I—I suppose. I don't really know." It was a shock to face the fact that she really didn't know what she wanted. She had thought that her affiliation with the orchestra here was the most important thing in her life, and she had been so wrong. Because of her blind devotion and self-absorption in music, she had lost the most important aspect of her life—David. She had stubbornly refused to believe that anything could be more important than her music, and because of her careless disregard for David and his feelings, she had lost both her job and him.

"What has happened to you?" Alexi's voice had taken on that familiar superciliousness. "I have a marvelous chance for you to work again. Now, let me hear your zealous little voice exclaim, 'How wonderful, Alexi!' " He effected a poor imitation of Elena's voice.

"All right," she laughed, deciding it was better to humor the man than argue with him. "How wonderful, Alexi!"

"That's better. Now, the orchestra is playing for the opera company's performance of *Hansel and Gretel* and the guest pianist who was scheduled for next week has canceled because he broke his ribs. Don't ask me how...you don't want to know. The point is, we are in dire straits and need someone who can play the score with a reasonable amount of style."

"Thanks a lot," Elena retorted.

"You know what I mean, *chérie*. Anyway, if you could come down here and play for us, I'm sure the directors—with my influence, of course—would undoubtedly hire you as a permanent fixture."

"Just what I always wanted to be," she murmured caustically.

"This is a big chance for you, Elena. Don't expect an offer like this to come along again or from anyone else. I know you. I know your limitations and weakness. I also know that you are reliable."

"Perhaps you didn't hear how badly I screwed up my last performance."

"Oh, I heard," he replied nonchalantly, and Elena could almost picture him waving his hand dismissively. "Now, can you make it by Friday?"

"Alexi! I haven't even said I would come."

"Of course you'll come. This is your life, Elena. I mean, really, dear, without the piano, what are you?"

Elena stared at the staff paper on which she had been scrawling and sighed. "Good question, Alexi. Damned good question."

"So, you call me when you have a flight scheduled and I will meet you at the airport. It's a dreadful city and you'll never find your way around. But you must be here by Friday morning so that we can rehearse."

"Oh, Alexi, I just don't know!"

"Do not say I don't know. Say I will call you when I have a flight. Now, good-bye, Elena."

"Good-bye, Alexi."

Chapter Thirteen

The plane dipped down through the clouds, making its less-than-graceful approach to Lambert Field.

Looking out her window, Elena could see in the distance the huge arch that perched at the bank of the Mississippi River, symbolizing the Gateway to the West.

As she began gathering her belongings, the gray-haired man next to her smiled. He watched her for a moment as she stuffed some sheet music into her satchel.

"Are you a musician?" He leaned toward her slightly as he spoke.

"Yes."

"That's wonderful. How lucky you are to have a talent like that."

She stared at the man for a long second, weighing his words in her mind. Lucky? No, that was one word she would never use to describe her talent.

Not for the first time Elena wondered what she was hoping to accomplish by coming here. Hadn't she messed up her life enough in the past few weeks? Coming to Saint Louis was probably only adding insult to injury.

"How long have you been a musician?" the man was asking her with polite interest.

"Forever," she answered dully, then immediately

looked contrite. "Well, actually, I guess it just seems that way. I've been playing professionally for about eight years." I've been a professional egoist for even longer than that, she wanted to add.

"What a sense of accomplishment you must feel." The man sighed and glanced at his own briefcase as if comparing his own life with Elena's.

Accomplishment! If that were not so pathetic, she might laugh. The only thing she had accomplished was to abuse an affectionate mother-daughter relationship and irreparably destroy the only love she had ever known with a man. She loved David more than anyone or anything else in the world. She realized that now. But she also knew that it was too late. She had dealt the killing blow that night at the concert hall.

"Do you write your own music?" The man was still interested, despite the fact that she had not responded to his last statement.

"I'm trying some things of my own, yes." She smiled, thinking about her finished composition. If there was an accomplishment in her life, it was that. She had finished it two days ago, added her lyrics, and packaged it in an envelope to mail to Dave. She hoped that, through this, he would know that she really did care.

There was a mild bump as the wheels touched pavement and then the loud roar of jet engines reversing their power.

As the plane taxied toward the gate, the older man leaned down to gather his belongings, smiling for one last time at Elena.

Walking into the terminal with her leather case of

sheet music, Elena spotted Alexi in the crowd. His face held that same dictatorial expression that she remembered so well. She raised her hand in greeting, but Alexi only nodded.

"Now," he began without even greeting her. "We have to proceed directly to the hall for rehearsal. I have upset my schedule enough by coming out here to pick you up." Elena smiled to herself. Some people just never changed.

As they walked to the luggage terminal to pick up her bag, Alexi kept up a stream of dialogue about the orchestra, the directors, the music hall, the audience.

"It's not the same here, Elena. You will learn this very quickly. The audience is not nearly so tolerant of a mediocre performance as they were in the East." Alexi swept his right hand back across his silver hair. "These midwestern pioneers can get hostile if things are not done their way."

"Hey, don't forget I went to school in this state."

Alexi glanced at her as if he were seeing her for the first time. "Why, for heaven's sake!"

"All I want to know," Elena laughed, glancing with amusement at Alexi as they walked, "is whether there are any child prodigies hanging in the wings."

"There are no Tinas, if that's what you're wondering. And heaven forbid if I should have to run into one more Eunice Buchanan."

After they picked up her suitcase, Alexi led her to a limousine that was waiting to take them to the music hall. "They may be pioneers—" Alexi shrugged when Elena looked thoroughly impressed "—but they do things in style."

When they arrived at the auditorium, the members

of the opera cast were in full costume for the afternoon dress rehearsal. Elena couldn't help but become caught up in the excitement of the theater. Alexi introduced her to his new orchestra, and then she sat down at the brown Baldwin to the left of the orchestra.

Elena ran her fingers up and down the keyboard to get a feel for the piano. She ran through the scales and chords and trailed her thumb down the keys in a glissando. After aligning her music in front of her, she began playing through the prayer from Act II of the opera.

The dress rehearsal lasted for four hours, and when it was over, Alexi instructed Elena on some tempo changes. By the time practice was ended, she was thoroughly exhausted and wanted nothing more than to find a nice soft bed into which she could crawl.

"I've found you a little apartment not far from here," Alexi told her as they headed back to the limousine. "It's only a studio flat, but it should serve your purposes until you can find something on your own."

Her purposes, she sighed. What were her purposes? Was this all there was for her: another city, another symphony? Playing for this orchestra for several years until she was once again replaced? How long would the pattern repeat itself before she grew old—alone? She leaned back against the thick upholstery of the limousine and closed her eyes. For the first time in her life Elena was genuinely afraid of what the future held for her.

Dave hung up his parka in the closet and opened his suitcase on the bed. Throwing out all of the dirty clothes onto the floor, he thought back over the trip. It had been nice skiing again after so many years. And there had been some isolated moments of fun with the group of people who had gone. Even with Kristin there had been times when he was glad he was there. But, on the whole, the trip had left him feeling more empty than before he went.

He tried to imagine what it would be like to go skiing with Elena. He smiled as he pictured trying to teach her to stand up on her skis, to snowplow, to sit on the lift properly. Wiping the thought away, he brusquely poured out the remainder of the contents from his suitcase onto the bed.

He looked with discontent around his new apartment. He had finally given up trying to find a house he wanted and had leased an apartment before he left for Vail. Expelling a heavy sigh, he wondered what the future held for him. Two weeks ago he was feeling so secure. He had a new job and he had Elena. What a mistake it had been to lean against such a false security.

After closing the empty suitcase and setting it in the back of the closet, he went to his desk and began methodically working his way through the mail. As he absently opened the stack of bills and junk mail, he thought about Elena, wondering what she was doing now. Was she depressed over the loss of her job? Maybe she was looking for a position somewhere else. Did she ever think about him? No! Dave shook his head to dispel the absurd notion. She had made it quite clear that their relationship had meant nothing to her.

He picked up a large manila envelope from the pile of mail and read the return address. Elena's address! He tore into the package, pulling out a small stack of staff paper that had been clipped together. A tiny note, unsigned, was attached to the upper left-hand corner. It read: "I was wrong."

Dave scanned through the pages, reading the lyrics she had added to her music. He devoured each word, remembering the notes she had played for him that day at her house. It was almost as if the words were meant for him. "Too late I learned what you already knew—that love can fill the day—like nothing else on earth can do."

He stared at the papers now shaking in his hands. What did this mean? Was this her way of saying that— that she really did care? He had promised himself that he would stop thinking about her, stop caring about her. But this—this gift that she had given him changed all of that. He had to call her. After all, it would be rude not to at least thank her for the piece.

Before a single doubt was allowed entrance into his mind, he was dialing her number, counting with despair the unanswered rings.

"The performance was marvelous, Miss Shubert." The executive director of the symphony was beaming at her. "Mr. Zsarkof did not do you justice. You play brilliantly."

"Thank you, Mr. Davis," Elena smiled politely, hoping she sounded more genuinely pleased than she actually was.

"The directors will be meeting Saturday, but I can assure you that I will recommend you as a permanent member of this orchestra. Of course, all negotiations will be through your manager."

Alexi watched closely as Elena's mouth curved into a hollow smile. What was the matter with her? She acted so indifferent over the director's compliments. She did not seem the least bit enthusiastic about this position. Didn't she realize how lucky she was to have this chance? He narrowed his gaze on her in speculation. Something about her complacent attitude was definitely not right.

When Elena left the concert hall for her studio apartment, she thought about what the executive director had said. Most likely she would be offered a position with this orchestra before the week was out. It was a chance that was almost too good to be true. She had believed that no other symphony organization would pick her up once she lost her other position. Of course, Alexi had quite a bit to do with it. If it weren't for him, she never would have been invited here in the first place.

She should be overjoyed! And yet, she wasn't. She tried to muster some honest enthusiasm for this position, but it was sorely lacking.

She kept thinking about David, wondering what he was doing, who he was seeing. Maybe the woman who had answered his phone was now at the center of his life. Elena felt a stab of pain as she thought of the woman, knowing the beauty of Dave's touch on her skin. Did she run her hands across the muscles of his back and chest? Did she know the power of his body at one with hers?

Elena shook her head to thrust the unwanted thoughts from creeping into her conscious mind. Jealousy for this unknown woman billowed within her, and with it came an unquenchable longing for the only man she had ever loved. What was she going to do without him?

Passing a delicatessen, she looked up dejectedly, remembering that day when Dave had given her her first driving lesson. In a fit of sentimentality she stepped through the doorway and ordered a pint of potato salad and some ham. If only he were here, they could buy mounds of food together and have a picnic in a park. She could lie back idly in the grass and listen to his deep voice, and feel his quiet presence, and do absolutely nothing of consequence all day.

Elena sighed with self-pity and loneliness. Resigning herself to the fact that she would probably have to eat the rest of her meals alone, she took the bag of food from the man behind the counter.

While he walked to the cash register to ring up her charges, he continued his conversation with another customer. They were talking football, so at first Elena payed no attention. But when they mentioned that a post-season game here this weekend was going to be televised, she listened more closely.

"Excuse me?" she interrupted. "I'm sorry, but do you happen to know who is going to be announcing that game?"

The customer and the man behind the counter looked at each other quizzically, wondering why anyone would care who was announcing a game. "I suppose Howard and Don," the customer said.

"No." Elena shook her head vigorously. "I mean the—the— Oh, I can't remember what it's called. I'm talking about the person who tells what the players are doing on the field."

"You mean the play-by-play?" the man behind the counter asked.

"Yes, that's it!" she sighed heavily, relieved to have gotten across her cryptic message.

"How should we know, lady? Why don't you call the stadium office? They might know."

Trying to hide her disappointment, she smiled. "All right, thank you. I'll do that."

After paying the man, she hurried down the sidewalk to her apartment. Throwing the now forgotten sack of food onto the table, she called directory assistance to get the number for the stadium office, then dialed the number with trembling fingers.

The secretary in the office was as surprised by Elena's question as the two men at the store had been. But she did promise to check for her.

Holding the phone while the secretary asked whoever else was in the office, Elena tried to calm her anxious breath. If only...if only—

"Hello?" the secretary greeted as she picked up the phone again. "Are you still there?"

"Yes." Elena closed her eyes tightly, waiting to hear what the secretary would say.

"Sorry it took so long, but I did find out for you. The play-by-play announcer will be Dave Atwell."

Elena tried to release the breath she had been holding, but it stuck. David was going to be here! He was going to be in Saint Louis! "Thank you," she croaked over the phone. "Thank you so much."

Elena pulled her pink cashmere sweater on over her head as she heard the knock at her door. Fastening her hair back from her face with a barrette, she opened the door to an impatient Alexi.

"Where have you been all morning? I've been trying to reach you on the telephone for hours."

"I went for a walk," Elena answered, gathering up her purse and checking to make sure she had her ticket.

"You've been walking for three hours?" He sounded perturbed that anyone would indulge in such a useless pursuit for fifteen minutes, much less three hours.

"That's right, Alexi." Elena slipped the purse strap onto her shoulder and thrust her other hand into the pocket of her gray corduroy jeans.

"Well, the directors are waiting to see you," he explained peevishly. "They want to talk over a position with you. So I've come to take you to them."

"Sorry, Alexi, but I have plans."

"Plans! What kind of plans? You can't have plans when the directors of the symphony want to talk to you."

"I'm going to a football game."

Alexi stared at her as if she had gone stark raving mad. "You must be joking!"

"Not in the least."

"Elena, I am talking about your career. You cannot expect the directors to understand that a football game is more important than what they have to offer you."

"You say football as if it were a dirty word," Elena retorted arrogantly.

"Well, look at the Neanderthals who play that barbaric sport. What could possibly be the attraction for such uncivilized behavior is beyond me. Besides, you have no idea how much trouble I went to to get you this opportunity."

"I know that, Alexi. And I really appreciate it, but I'm just not interested."

"You mean, you don't want the position?" He was aghast that anyone in her right mind would turn down such an opportunity with a major city symphony.

"That's right. I don't want the position."

"I—I thought music was your life?" A huffy tone of arrogance had crept into his voice.

Elena sighed, knowing how difficult it must be for Alexi to understand how she felt. She wasn't even sure if she understood her own feelings. It was just that she had come to realize that life wasn't as narrowly defined as she once believed it to be. A person did have choices. There were different paths and crossroads at which to turn.

"Music will always be a big part of my life, Alexi. But...I know now that it is not my entire life."

"What else is?" His voice was a reflection of his scorn for this type of thinking. "What else can be when you are an artist?"

"That is precisely what I have to find out. Do you realize that I am almost thirty-one years old and I still don't know who I am."

"Oh, really, Elena." He was now thoroughly disgusted. "You sound more like an eighteen-year-old sapling than a mature woman. This is the most ridiculous—"

"You say I'm like an eighteen-year-old, Alexi. Well, that is precisely when I closed the door on the rest of the world. I have to go back and reopen it. I have to try to let in all the things that I've missed."

"If you turn down this offer, you will never get another. You do realize that, don't you?"

"Yes. I know that."

As Alexi slammed the door with a resounding crash, Elena felt a sudden surge of freedom wash over her, such as she had never known in her life. She automatically thought back to the days of practicing hour upon hour at the piano, of growing up by the open window. She breathed in the heady scent of honeysuckle, and she knew that she was finally alive and utterly free.

Chapter Fourteen

"For a benefit, that was one hell of a game."

"Yeah, but I tell you what, I was sweating as much as if I were on the field."

"That reminds me, you owe me twenty bucks."

"Yeah, yeah, yeah. Don't rub it in."

The press box buzzed with post-game activity. Announcers gathered up their statistic sheets, wadded up scratch paper, tossing it into overflowing trash cans, and swept pencils into briefcases with their hands. As they talked they drained the dregs of coffee and crunched up the paper cups, pitching them into the wastebaskets.

In contrast, Dave stacked his papers neatly and laid them in his briefcase, closing and latching the lid securely. He was quieter than the others were, but they chalked up his sullen mood to fatigue. He had had to work extra hard to keep up with the teams in this game.

One of the men in the press box lifted his binoculars to his eyes, scanning the stadium for one last time.

"The clean-up crew is sure going to be busy tomorrow picking up all those popcorn boxes and programs." He moved the binoculars in a line across the benches. He stopped, then backed up to a figure that caught his attention. "That chick over there must be really upset about the game." The binoculars were focused on a lone figure on the far side of the stadium.

"A sore loser, you think?" laughed another announcer.

"Well—" the man with the binoculars tried to focus better "—either that or she's asleep. She's not moving!"

"Maybe somebody brought one of those blow-up dolls with him to the—"

"Let me take a look." Dave finally laughed along with the others, reaching for the glasses.

He lifted the binoculars to his eyes, readjusting the focus to accommodate his vision, then skimmed along the rows until the figure was in sight. He pulled the glasses away from his eyes, frowning as he stared at the tiny figure so far away. He lifted the binoculars back up to his eyes for another look.

"What do you think, Atwell? Does she look like something you'd want to take home for a midnight snack?"

"Hell, if it's that interesting, let me take a look." Another man walked over to reach for the glasses.

Dave jerked away, still holding them in front of his eyes. Ignoring the comments around him, he trained every nerve of concentration on the small figure as she wrapped her arms around her body for warmth.

She was wearing a crocheted tam, and thick waves of russet hair were falling over the gray coat wrapped tightly around her body. She moved for the first time since he began looking at her through the binoculars. As she turned her head to the side and swept her hair back, he got the first clear glimpse of her face.

Slowly, and in a daze, he lowered the glasses to the counter, frowning through the window with disbelief. Elena here at the game!

His insides began to tremble as he tried to make sense of her presence. What was she doing in Saint Louis? What was she doing at the game? Surely she hadn't come here for that reason alone. But why?

He had tried so many times to call her since he received her composition in the mail. But she had never answered. He had even checked with the executive director of the symphony for any news of her whereabouts, but he had had no information. He had finally decided that she must have gone to visit her mother in California. But Saint Louis! Never in a million years would he have dreamed of seeing her here.

"Where are you going, Atwell?" Several eyes were trained on him as he slipped on his jacket.

"I think he's going to go check out that action over there." One of the men pointed to the lone figure in the bleachers.

"Well, good luck, man." Dave ignored the offers of cheer as he opened the door of the press box that led to the stands.

He could have taken the elevator down and then walked around the field, but that way was too quick. He needed time to think, to evaluate what was happening to him, what he wanted to say to her.

Elena lifted her head, watching the small figure climbing down from the press box, walking down the steps of the opposite bleachers from where she sat. It could be David. It was possible that he could have seen her here. But then, that would be too much to hope for.

And if it was him, what would she say to him? He might not accept her apology if she gave him one. He could very easily spurn any attempts she might make at an apology. What would she say when he asked her why she had come here? She didn't even know the answer to that one herself.

Her pulse began to accelerate as he climbed over the railing and down onto the playing field.

When he first set foot on the sidelines, an indefinable feeling swept over him. Memories engulfed him and dragged him away from the present. As he walked slowly across the field, he heard the crowd cheering, the loudspeaker singing with the play-by-play. He was in the huddle listening to the quarterback. He moved to his position in the T-formation. He wiped the sweat from his palms, his pulse racing with a mixture of excitement and fear. He heard the snap, hesitated for just a moment, saw the play developing, then charged forward at full speed to take the handoff.

Dave had the ball. He could see the line open up in front of him, and he was running free. In those few brief moments he was buffeted from the rest of the world in his own surrealistic, slow-moving silence. He could feel his heart pounding, his breath labored and painful in his chest. His legs were carrying him, knowing there were opposing players on his tail, gaining on him, moving in for the tackle. Panting now, he forced his legs to move faster, drawing closer and closer to the goal line. By this time the crowd was feverish with excitement. But all Dave could hear was his breath and his feet as they hit the ground, the groans behind him, the crunching of helmets and shoulder pads.

As suddenly as the shout from the past had thundered through his mind, it quieted. Dave looked at the empty field he was crossing, the silence almost deafening by now. He was strangely detached from it all, feeling like an outsider. It struck him with quiet resignation that he no longer belonged here. His place was no longer on the field; it was in the press box.

He glanced up at Elena as he climbed over the railing on her side of the stands, and he smiled. He would love to tell her what he just discovered within himself. That moving from one phase of one's life to another was not so bad after all. Oh, but she probably wouldn't understand. She had not yet discovered that the closing of one door always meant the opening of another.

Elena watched him climbing up the steps toward her. Her heart was palpitating with a mixture of excitement and apprehension. There was so much she wanted to tell David. So much she wanted him to understand about her. How she had changed, how she had come to understand some basic things about herself. She was aware that she still had a long way to go until she knew who Elena Shubert was. But at least she had taken the first step. And yet, would David understand that? Would he be able to discern any change in her at all?

Dave stopped, two steps below Elena. He stared at

her and she at him. A huge chasm had been dug between them and one of them was going to have to
make an attempt to cross it. He climbed one step
higher.

He was close enough to touch her. He wanted to
reach out and run his fingers through that thick hair.
He wanted to smile. He wanted to say something!
But his tongue was stuck to the roof of his mouth as
if it were glued there.

She tried to force her mouth into a smile, but it
wouldn't move. What if she smiled and he didn't
return it? Why couldn't she make the words she had
been formulating all afternoon spill from her mouth?
She felt like an idiot!

"Elena?" Dave groaned inwardly. *God, how stupid I sound. Of course it's Elena.*

"Hi, David." Both of their mouths were drawn
tightly, as if each was afraid to initiate the first
smile.

"What are you doing here?" Oh, why was he asking that? Who cared why she was here; he was just
happy that she was.

He was asking the one question she didn't know
how to answer. She had felt a compulsion to come,
but she could not define its source. "To see you,"
she answered, startling herself with the truth.

"You came all the way to Saint Louis just to see
me?"

"Well, I've been here for about a week. I was playing with the local symphony."

"Oh." So she had found another orchestra to hire
her. He was sure she must be happy, so he tried to
muster some enthusiasm. "That's great!"

"Not really," she answered, watching him carefully. He was guarding his features so closely, she
couldn't tell what he was thinking. "They. . . I think
they want me to stay on with the orchestra."

"Great!" he repeated, forcing his jaw into a
tighter clench. So she would be staying in Saint
Louis. She must have come to the game to tell him
that. Why didn't she just call him if she wanted him
to know that badly?

"Alexi told me— You remember Alexi Zsarkof,
don't you?"

Dave nodded.

"He came to my apartment today and told me the
directors wanted to offer me a position. He had come
to take me to them. I told him I was coming to the
football game instead."

Dave's eyes widened noticeably, but his mouth was
still held in check. "Don't you think that might make
them angry that you found the game more important
than their offer?"

"Yes. But then, I did think it was more important." She glanced down at her hands clasped tightly
in her lap. She was too afraid to look into his eyes.
She couldn't bear to see his disdain or, even worse,
his laughter.

Dave watched the pulse in her neck pounding er-
ratically, as if she were afraid. Was she afraid of
him? "I don't understand," he said, not wanting to
read anything into her words that weren't there.

"I guess, in effect, I turned down the position."

"Why?"

"Well, like you said to me, I had lingered too long
in the chambers of the sea. You gave me a glimpse of

what I had been missing, and. . . I liked the world you showed me. I want to see more.''

"You mean you don't want to play for any symphony?''

"No, I don't think so. It's too all-consuming. And I made a big enough mess with the last one I was with.''

"Your mistake at the concert was understandable, Elena.''

"That's not what I meant. I mean, because of my absorption in my music, I made a mess of. . .us.'' She finally looked up at him, forcing her eyes to meet his head on. If she was expecting derision in his expression, it was lacking. His eyes shone brightly in the fading light, as if he were opening a door into his inner feelings.

Dave bridged the final gap, stepping up even with her and sitting beside her on the bleacher. He rested his elbows on his knees, his hands clasped in front of him. "I was an idiot to threaten your conductor, Elena. That was probably one of the most childish things I've ever done.''

She smiled at his forlorn profile and wanted to run her hand through his tousled hair. "It's okay, David. I didn't appreciate what you did at the time, but now—''

He turned his head sideways to look at her. "What changed your mind?''

"I realized that my music was nothing compared to what we had. David, I'm so sorry.'' She began to cry. "I'm so sorry.''

Enclosing her in his arms, he held her head against his chest. "It's okay, Elena. It's okay. I was too stubborn to see what you were going through. I guess I wanted you to come crawling back to me.'' He laughed bitterly. ''How long could we have stayed away from each other?'' he added on an introspective note.

''I tried to call you one night.''

''Really? And I wasn't there?'' He froze, wondering what she would think of him when he told her about the ski trip.

Elena paused, afraid to go on lest she learn what she most dreaded to hear. ''I'm sure you were there.''

''I don't understand.''

''A woman answered your phone.''

''A woman? There has been no woman in my—'' Dave stopped, dumbstruck by the memory that assailed him. The night he had gone for the ice. The other three had stayed in his room. He had heard a telephone ringing. Oh, no, it must have been Elena, and Kristin was sitting closest to the phone.

Elena glanced up at David, wondering if he was going to lie to her. She saw the look of frozen panic on his face and held her breath.

''There was a woman there,'' he answered solemnly. ''Her name is Kristin.''

God! Don't tell me her name. I don't want to know! Now she had a name to put to the body that had known David's body, who had held him through the night. A name to match the sultry voice over the phone.

Dave looked at Elena's tightly clamped lips as she tried to conceal her emotions. But he saw her eyes. The pain she felt was clearly evident in the moist gray irises. Puffing out his cheeks, he expelled a long, pensive sigh.

"Do you remember the day I told you not to use me as an implement for your physical needs?"

Elena didn't answer. Her muscles were clenched too tightly to allow even the slightest movement.

"Well," he continued, knowing that she was listening, "that's what Kristin was to me, Elena. Nothing more than that."

Elena finally spoke, but her voice was so soft that Dave had to bend his head down to hear her. "I guess that there's something wrong with me, then. Maybe I should have gone right out and jumped into bed with the first guy who asked me."

"Who asked you?" Dave's voice and body tensed at the same moment.

Elena glanced upward, surprised by the brusque tone of his voice. Smiling a little wistfully, she answered truthfully, "No one."

Dave's body relaxed and he pulled her head back against his chest. "The entire male population is a bunch of fools, then. But," he laughed, "I have to admit, I'm grateful." Pausing, weighing his words very carefully, he spoke softly. "I want to be the first to ask you."

Elena tried to lift her head, but David's hand held it tightly to his chest. "Ask me what?" she whispered breathlessly, her body aching for his touch.

He finally moved his hand and tilted her head upward. His mouth moved in a soft caress across her lips, while he drank in the scent of her sweet fragrance. He was almost intoxicated from the heady wine of her nearness. His kiss became deeper, more passionate, and his arms snaked around her body, holding her fast against him. He buried his mouth in her neck, his words moving against her throat. "I've missed you so much, Elena. I've been like a drowning man."

She clung to him with her arms, tears of joy and tears of regret washing down her cheeks. "David, I was so foolish. I didn't know what I was saying or doing. I—"

His mouth silenced her apology, his tongue thrusting deep into her mouth as if he couldn't get enough of her.

She clenched his hair between her fingers, pulling and grasping and holding on to this man who lifted her to such unimaginable heights.

He pulled his mouth away from her, his breathing strained and rapid. "Come with me," he pleaded. "My car is in the parking lot."

Holding her hands, he lifted her to her feet and together they walked down the steps of the stadium and crossed the long, empty, and darkening field with their arms around each other's waists.

"You know—" he pulled her tighter against his side as they reached the goalpost "—I'm glad I'm not playing football anymore."

She glanced up at his face as he looked down at her. "Really?"

"I mean that. I like what I'm doing now. I've still got lots of years to find out what this world has to offer. I'm ready for a change."

"So am I, David. I never would have realized that

if it hadn't been for you. I never would have known what I was missing.''

When they finally reached his car, Elena was surprised to see that it was his Mercedes. "Did you drive here?"

"Yes. I have to go on to Oklahoma and Texas before I return, so I decided it would be more fun to drive than fly.'' He paused, his mind toying with an idea. "Would you want to come with me? I'll be gone about two and a half weeks.''

She looked up at his strong, masculine face, his windswept hair, his boyish eagerness, and she smiled. "I'd love to go with you. If you hadn't asked me, I probably would have stowed away in your trunk.''

Pressing her against the car, Dave kissed her tenderly and leisurely. Night had fallen around them and the parking lot was empty at this hour. They were lost in their own private world where no one existed but the two of them.

Dave unlocked the car, and Elena's eyes widened when he opened the back door. She looked up at him as he smiled mischievously. He leaned down close, whispering his words behind her ear. "Let's finish what we started twelve years ago.''

A shiver of anticipation and excitement rippled down her spine as she nodded her head. Elena climbed into the backseat, and before Dave followed, he inserted his key into the steering column, turning the key to the left. He then pushed a cassette into the tape deck and the soft, silvery sounds of "Clair de Lune'' fed the night.

Dave climbed into the backseat and closed the door. Pulling Elena toward him, he leaned against the door, with her back and hips snuggled against his chest and inner thighs.

"Won't you wear down your battery?" She let her head drop back onto his shoulder, as the music softened her soul.

Dave kissed the top of her head. "Honey, my battery is so charged up, it is going to take a lifetime to run down."

He wrapped his arms around her waist, his hand slowly gliding up to cup her breast, while he quoted Shakespeare: " 'Here we will sit, and let the sounds of music creep in our ears; soft stillness and the night become the touches of sweet harmony.' "

"With a poetic soul like that, you must have been a lousy football player," she teased lightly as she luxuriated in the feel of his hand lifting under her sweater.

"But I'm a great lover." His hand moved to unclasp the front of her bra while his teeth nibbled the side of her neck.

"I'll be the judge of that," she answered without a breath. His fingers were moving in circular motions across her breast, rolling the tip to a peak between his thumb and forefinger.

She shifted sideways, her body straining to join with his, and as his lips joined in a sweeping embrace with hers, a soft moan escaped her throat.

Dave's hands moved in fervent caresses across her back and hips, dipping down into the back waistband of her jeans. Elena's fingers were stroking his neck, trailing down his chest and side.

As their lips met once more, Dave rolled her beneath him on the seat, covering her body with his own. His hands ran wildly across her body, sending electrical impulses of need screaming through her bloodstream.

The sounds of "Intermezzo" wove through the interior of the car and Dave noticed that the windows were now covered with fog.

When he lifted her sweater, she looped her arms around his neck, pulling him down against her, his mouth open on her breast, his tongue moving in slow circles where his fingers had been. As he drew the stiffened peak inside his warm mouth, she arched her body upward, wanting to merge her flesh with his.

His free hand lifted her hips upward into his pelvis and she wrapped her legs around his thighs in an urgent plea.

"God, Elena. I've never felt with anyone the way I do with you. You set me on fire the same way you did when I was twenty." His tongue blazed a trail across her chest to her other breast.

Elena placed the palms of her hands on David's hips, urging him tighter against her, causing him to moan with desire.

Forcing his hand between them, he slowly lowered her zipper.

As their mouths fused, so did their bodies and their passion. The loving sounds that came from their throats mingled in the night, harmonizing tones that carried them to some faraway place where the moonlight, the music, and their bodies became one.

Afterward they clung to each other as if they had become life supports for one another, holding fast to the strength of arms and legs and united souls.

They lay together, their bodies entwined in the small confines of the car, and listened to the slow, rhythmic beat of each other's heart. Dave kissed Elena's neck and temples, her hair and eyes.

"Don't ever let me leave you again, David. Or say things I don't mean. Or—"

His mouth covered hers, smothering the words within her. "I won't," he spoke into her mouth as he kissed her. "I won't let you leave me again. I love you, Elena. I want to do what I should have done when I was twenty."

"What is that?" Her eyes smiled up into his.

"I want to marry you. I'll give you time to think about it," he hurried on. He couldn't stand it if she said no right now. "I just want you to know that—" This time, his words were cut off as she pulled his lips down onto hers, her tongue snaking into the warm, moist depths of his mouth.

"I don't want to think about it," she murmured against his face when she finally freed his mouth. "I want to marry you too."

The embrace that held them together for several minutes was a wordless caress of relief and security and dedication and love. They had both had their isolated moments of greatness apart, and now they were ready to forge a path through life together.

"We've got a lot to learn about each other," Dave reflected.

"And that big wide world out there too," she added. "But, David, I do want to keep my music alive." She had to make him understand that it was an integral part of her life.

"I wouldn't want you to do otherwise," he assured her. "In fact, I gave your song to this guy who is producing a Broadway musical and—"

"My song? The one I sent to you?" Elena's voice held the breathless excitement of a schoolgirl. "You know a producer?"

"Hey, I have connections," he laughed flippantly. "Well, actually—" he shrugged sheepishly "—I know a friend of a friend of a friend of the producer. But still, you never know."

"Oh, David, I love you so much!" Elena flung her arms around his neck. "There is so much we can learn from each other."

"I'm a very willing pupil too." He snuggled deeper against her. "Why don't you teach me everything you know." His mouth dipped down to her throat.

"The only things I know—" she gasped as his tongue began an intimate exploration of her breasts and stomach "—are...scales—"

"Yes," he murmured against the flesh of her lower abdomen, his tongue striking the passionate keys deep within her.

As she closed her eyes she drank in the pleasure from his mouth and tongue, her nerve endings awakening to a new symphony of sensations.

"And I know about chords," she sighed, trembling with the sonorous harmony that lifted her spirit closer to his.

As he lowered himself onto her once more, he cupped her face in his hands, smiling into her eyes. "I want to know every note and every possible chord within you."

"If you are a dedicated lover...of music—" she

smiled softly "—then you must devote long hours to study and practice."

"I am definitely dedicated. If this is what my practice sessions will be like, there won't be enough hours in the day."

"Then maybe we'd better get started with your first lesson," she advised, lifting her hips provocatively into his.

"Yes," he agreed with a ragged breath, easing his body into position with hers. "As they say, practice makes perfect."

"I can tell you're going to be a most gifted pupil," she sighed.

"Only because I have an enchanting virtuoso who will keep me spellbound with her music forever."

"Then by all means—" she stopped, almost crying out with the thrill of David's body in absolute harmony with her own "—let the music begin."

Elena ran out of the building that housed the Department of Motor Vehicles, waving her new driver's license with excitement. Jumping into the car with Dave, she laughed jubilantly. "Now I know what it must feel like to be sixteen years old. This is so exciting! My own driver's license." She narrowed her eyes on David's serious expression. "What's the matter with you?"

"I'm thinking about what the government has just unleashed on an unsuspecting public." He was trying hard to keep his mouth in a straight line.

"You mean me?" she asked innocently.

He finally smiled. "I mean you. Didn't the instructor in there ask you if you learned to drive through a correspondence course?''

"No." She tossed her head saucily. "I told him that you taught me."

"And?"

She smiled mischievously. "He said he certainly hoped I drove better than you played football."

"He didn't!" Dave exploded with mock anger.

"No, he didn't," she answered pertly.

Dave grabbed Elena, pulling her next to his chest while he growled against her neck. Wrapping one arm around his broad shoulders, she held her other hand up to the window, where the light glinted brightly on the gold band around her third finger. She sighed, aware of the joy that seemed to increase more each day since they had married almost a year ago.

"So." She leaned her head upon his shoulder. "Now we have two things to celebrate. The renewal of your sports announcing contract and my new driver's license."

"Honey, you know that means I'm going to have to keep traveling, don't you?"

"I know, but I'll keep busy with the musical. I still can't believe I'm going to be assisting Bob Davis on the score! I just hope I can meet their expectations of me."

"Don't worry about letting them down, honey. They're going to love you." Dave was beaming with pride over Elena's musical talent. "After all, I love you, and I'm a great judge of character."

"No one could love me half as much as you do,

David.'' Elena's liquid gray eyes were full of the wonder she had come to know with him.

He cupped her face in his hands. "You're right about that. No one will ever love you as much as I do."

Elena closed her eyes, feeling the all-encompassing embrace of his love. David had known from the beginning. They were like a duet, each having his and her own notes to play, but together comprising a symphony of silver sounds so full of love it would fill all the moonlit nights of their lives.

Take these 4 best-selling novels FREE

Yes! Four sophisticated, contemporary love stories by four world-famous authors of romance FREE, as your introduction to the Harlequin Presents subscription plan. Thrill to **Anne Mather**'s passionate story BORN OUT OF LOVE, set in the Caribbean.... Travel to darkest Africa in **Violet Winspear**'s TIME OF THE TEMPTRESS....Let **Charlotte Lamb** take you to the fascinating world of London's Fleet Street in MAN'S WORLD .... Discover beautiful Greece in **Sally Wentworth**'s moving romance SAY HELLO TO YESTERD.

Harlequin Presents...

The very finest in romance fiction

Join the millions of avid Harlequin readers all over the world who delight in the magic of a really exciting novel. EIGHT great NEW titles published EACH MONTH! Each month you will get to know exciting, interesting, true-to-life people .... You'll be swept to distant lands you'\\ dreamed of visiting .... Intrigue, adventure, romance, and the destiny of many lives will thrill you through each Harlequin Presents novel.

Get all the latest books before they're sold out!
As a Harlequin subscriber you actually receive your personal copies of the latest Presents novels immediately after they come off the press, so you're sure of getting all , 8 each month.

Cancel your subscription whenever you wish!
You don't have to buy any minimum number of books. Whenever you decide to stop your subscription just let us know and we'll cancel all further shipments.

Now's your chance to discover the earlier
books in this exciting series.

Choose from this list of great

SUPERROMANCES!

SUPER**ROMANCE**

Complete and mail this coupon today!

Worldwide Reader Service

In the U.S.A.
1440 South Priest Drive
Tempe, AZ 85281

In Canada
649 Ontario Street
Stratford, Ontario N5A 6W2

Please send me the following SUPERROMANCES. I am enclosing my check or money order for $2.50 for each copy ordered, plus 75¢ to cover postage and handling.

☐ # 26	☐ # 32	☐ # 38
☐ # 27	☐ # 33	☐ # 39
☐ # 28	☐ # 34	☐ # 40
☐ # 29	☐ # 35	☐ # 41
☐ # 30	☐ # 36	
☐ # 31	☐ # 37	

Number of copies checked @ $2.50 each = $_____
N.Y. and Ariz. residents add appropriate sales tax $_____
Postage and handling $_____ .75

                               TOTAL $_____

I enclose _____
(Please send check or money order. We cannot be responsible for cash sent through the mail.)
Prices subject to change without notice.   Offer expires January 31, 1984

NAME_____
                         (Please Print)

ADDRESS_____APT. NO. _____

CITY_____

STATE/PROV._____

ZIP/POSTAL CODE_____

30756000000

Just what the woman on the go needs!

BOOK MATE

The perfect "mate" for all Harlequin paperbacks
Traveling • Vacationing • At Work • In Bed • Studying
• Cooking • Eating

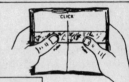
Pages turn WITHOUT opening the strap.

Perfect size for all standard paperbacks, this wonderful invention makes reading a pure pleasure! Ingenious design holds paperback books OPEN and FLAT so even wind can't ruffle pages— leaves your hands free to do other things. Reinforced, wipe-clean vinyl-covered holder flexes to let you turn pages without undoing the strap...supports paperbacks so well, they have the strength of hardcovers!

SEE-THROUGH STRAP
Reinforced back stays flat.

Built in bookmark

BOOK MARK
BACK COVER HOLDING STRIP

10" x 7¼", opened.
Snaps closed for easy carrying, too.

Available now. Send your name, address, and zip or postal code, along with a check or money order for just $4.99 + .75 ¢ for postage & handling (for a total of $5.74) payable to Harlequin Reader Service to:

Harlequin Reader Service

In U.S.
P.O. Box 22188
Tempe, AZ 85282

In Canada
649 Ontario Street
Stratford, Ont. N5A 6W2

HARLEQUIN CLASSIC LIBRARY

Great old romance classics from our early publishing lists.

On the following page is a coupon with which you may order any or all of these titles. If you order all nine, you will receive a FREE book—*District Nurse,* a heartwarming classic romance by Lucy Agnes Hancock.

The fourteenth set of nine novels in the

HARLEQUIN CLASSIC LIBRARY

LUCY AGNES HANCOCK

District Nurse

118 **Then Come Kiss Me** Mary Burchell
119 **Towards the Dawn** Jane Arbor
120 **Homeward the Heart** Elizabeth Hoy
121 **Mayenga Farm** Kathryn Blair
122 **Charity Child** Sara Seale
123 **Moon at the Full** Susan Barrie
124 **Hope for Tomorrow** Anne Weale
125 **Desert Doorway** Pamela Kent
126 **Whisper of Doubt** Andrea Blake

VV G +

Great old favorites...
Harlequin Classic Library
Complete and mail this coupon today!

FREE BONUS BOOK

Harlequin Reader Service

In U.S.A.
1440 South Priest Drive
Tempe, AZ 85281

In Canada
649 Ontario Street
Stratford, Ontario N5A 6W2

Please send me the following novels from the Harlequin Classic Library. I am
enclosing my check or money order for $1.50 for each novel ordered, plus 75¢
to cover postage and handling. If I order all nine titles at one time, I will receive
a FREE book, *District Nurse,* by Lucy Agnes Hancock.

- ☐ 118
- ☐ 119
- ☐ 120
- ☐ 121
- ☐ 122
- ☐ 123
- ☐ 124
- ☐ 125
- ☐ 126

Number of novels checked @ $1.50 each = $_____

N.Y. and Ariz. residents add appropriate sales tax $_____

Postage and handling $_____.75

TOTAL $_____

I enclose _____
(Please send check or money order. We cannot be responsible for cash sent
through the mail.)
Prices subject to change without notice.   Offer expires January 31, 1984

Name _____
               (Please Print)

Address _____
                              (Apt. no.)

City _____

State/Prov. _____

Zip/Postal Code _____

30756000000